COWBOY'S MATCH

COWBOY'S
MATCH

LEXI POST

Cowboy's Match

Two Hearts, Two Fires...

Cowboy Cole Hatcher became a firefighter to support his horse rescue ranch. He never dreamed it would lead him back to his first love, but a fire at the Poker Flat Nudist Resort lands him face-to-face with Lacey Winters. She may have started the fire that ended their relationship, but the sight of her reignites his long buried feelings.

Lacey is shocked the hunky firefighter is the same man who dumped her eight years ago. Cole burned Lacey in the past when he failed to stand by her and she's determined not to let him back into her heart. But everything about the new Cole is just too hot to resist. He melts her defenses, sweeping her away into a night of erotic passion only to rip open old wounds.

Determined to prove who set the Poker Flat fire and the original fire that destroyed their relationship, Cole investigates both, unearthing ugly truths that reveal even more damage. Now, he's not sure he can catch the arsonist or the heart of the woman he never stopped loving.

Acknowledgments

Thanks to my better half, Chief Robert Fabich, Sr., for his invaluable help and knowledge of arson, fires and fire suppression. I learned so much…as usual.

For Paige Wood, who really enjoyed this story and keeps the pressure on for me to write the next one. And for my mom, Jo Brous, who came up with the title when I was at a complete loss.

Thank you to Spur Cross Stables in Cave Creek, Arizona for accepting less than perfect horses for trail rides and for allowing me to visit. I especially have to thank the Spur Cross Stables head wrangler Boot (his real name) for spending hours answering all my questions and introducing me to their wonderful horses.

Of course, I dragged my critique partner, Marie Patrick, out to the ranch as well and she was so patient (and learned a lot, too). I struck gold when I met up with her. Last, I'd like to thank Merritt Crowder for her sharp eye and excellent vocabulary.

I couldn't ask for better resources on this story. Any incorrect information is completely the fault of the author.

AUTHOR'S NOTE

Cowboy's Match was inspired by Bret Harte's short story, *The Outcasts of Poker Flat*, first published in 1869. In Harte's story, four members of Poker Flat society—a gambler, a prostitute, a madam, and a drunk--are banned from the western settlement when a sudden urge to be virtuous overtakes the citizens. On their way to the next settlement, the outcasts stop to rest at the base of some high mountains. An innocent couple, a young man and his fiancée (a tavern waitress), comes down from the mountains and rests with them. This cast of characters explores the relationship between the innocent and the tainted in Harte's story.

But what if the lines blur and it becomes unclear who is innocent and who is tainted? Can love become the fire by which the truth is revealed?

CHAPTER ONE

Cole Hatcher ignored the yellow and orange streaks of the Arizona sunset and focused on the same colors rising from the burning building as flames moved with the breeze. He spoke into the radio. "Move the two and a half inch to the northwest corner."

Two firefighters lugged the hose toward the base of the fire at the edge of the partially constructed building. Not more than fifteen feet away was a pile of old barn wood just waiting to ignite.

Stepping back toward the engine, Cole received a nod from Mason, the fire engine monitor, before speaking into the radio again. "Tanker, is the dry hydrant hooked yet?"

"Almost." The reply was not the answer Cole wanted. They would need more water than an engine and tanker could provide, and the chance of the winds picking up once the sun disappeared were better than a horse getting loose through an open gate.

As if on cue, the whinny of several frightened horses in the nearby barn caused him to tense. There was no way he would let the fire spread that way.

The radio clicked before a firefighter's voice came through. "We're hooked."

Cole breathed easier. As long as he had water, he could put this baby out. "Good. Stay with the tanker. I'll need someone to come over here and grab the one and a half inch with Clark." He watched as Clark unwound the hose, already heading toward the construction site that hid behind the smoke and flames of the fire's onslaught.

Glancing back to where the tanker was parked thirty yards away, Cole swore. "What the hell?" Coming up the hill along the dirt road his trucks had just rolled in on, were at least a half dozen golf carts filled with naked people.

He stifled a laugh. What'd they think this was? A campfire? A Wild West show? Did they plan to make s'mores? This would be a story to tell at the firehouse for sure. Still, as with all spectators to a disaster, it wasn't safe for them to be there. He silently wished he had a radio to communicate with the owner, who had enough sense to keep the resort guests from getting any closer.

For over a year, he'd been curious about the Poker Flat Nudist Resort, but Clark had been chosen to give the fire extinguisher class to all the employees before the resort opened three months ago, and Cole had no official reason to come check it out. Fighting a fire wasn't a good way to learn about a place. Whatever this new construction was, it was toast. His concern was with the barn and the horses and which way the wind would blow next.

An explosion from the fire shook the ground as flames shot into the air. "Shit." What the hell did they have in that unfinished building? The two men with the smaller hose lost their footing and fell, but since they hadn't made it to the fire yet, they were unharmed.

He'd be damned if he'd put his men in harm's way when no lives were at stake.

He turned toward the owner and motioned her closer, then faced the burning construction site. As the sky behind the fire turned a dull pink, the breeze picked up, changing the direction of the flames toward the open desert. Good for the horses, but not for wildfire potential. It'd been the driest summer on record. October temperature highs had finally dropped below triple digits and the nights were already getting cold, but there had been no rain during monsoon season.

Cole spoke into the radio again. "I need the two and half inch to lay down a curtain between the building and the open desert on your side."

"Got it." The two firefighters adjusted their hose and started a continual spray, wetting and cooling the area toward the open desert even as the men with the one and a half inch hose moved in to cover the fire base.

"Lieutenant, you wanted us?" The female voice had him turning around.

He'd forgotten he'd called over the owner. At least she and the cowboy with her were dressed. "You need to get those people out of here. I can't control the fire's embers and right now the wind is picking up."

The tall man nodded. "I'll take care of that." He immediately strode toward the golf cart brigade.

Cole turned his attention to the woman. "I've got my men focused on keeping the fire from spreading to your barn or out into the desert. A wildfire would be catastrophic, but we won't be able to save the building."

She waved her hand as if it meant little to her. "I'm not worried about the building as long as everyone is safe."

"Have you accounted for all your employees and guests?"

"Yes."

Another explosion had Cole turning away to check on his men. A voice came across his radio. "What the fuck is in here? A chemical lab?"

Cole frowned. He'd never thought of how convenient it would be to have a meth lab out at a nudist resort. He'd make sure the police investigated the place in case there had been illegal activity.

He looked at the owner. "How many more explosions should we expect?"

She frowned. "We had one before you arrived, that's what alerted me to the fire, but there shouldn't be anything that would explode over there. The plywood for the roof was completed, but they hadn't even set the windows in yet. All that was there was whatever the construction crew left."

"Do you have electricity out there yet?"

She shook her head.

Shit. "Gasoline for their generator." He spoke into his radio again. "Possible gas containers."

A gust of wind compounded his problems and he quickly repositioned his men. A siren could barely be heard in the distance, but the red and blue lights of a sheriff department car reflected far into the desert. About time they got here.

Cole spared a glance to where the golf carts had been parked and was relieved to see only a few left, but he scowled as a young woman with golden hair moved toward him and the owner, a tray of food and drinks in her hands. Shit, didn't these people realize this was a working fire? This was dangerous!

A third explosion rocked the ground and he spun in time to see a gust of wind pick up the roiling flames and throw them toward his men. He pressed the button on his radio. "Fall back!"

One man stumbled backward, catching his foot on the old barn wood and lost his grip on the hose. The other firefighter struggled with it before he went down, too.

"Fuck." Cole sprinted to his men, pulling them back by their coats as the flames licked at their boots. The barn wood caught, feeding the fire.

Once his men were out of harm's way, he tackled the flailing line. A loose hose was a danger in its own right.

"Lieutenant, do you want us on the wood pile?" The question came through his radio.

Cole slammed his body onto the hose before replying, "Negative. Keep that curtain up."

The two firefighters that had been blown down regained their feet and grabbed the hose. "Thanks, Lieutenant."

He released his hold. "Pull back and soak that pile. If the wind shifts again, I don't want the barn catching."

The men nodded.

Cole turned around and strode back to the engine. The two women were still there. This wasn't a movie. Didn't they have any common sense?

After checking with Mason to be sure the water pressure was steady, he approached his audience, irritation growing at the petite stature of the blonde. Someone so delicate didn't belong at a working fire, but like the owner, at least she had clothes on. "Ladies, you need to get back." He pointed to the rise the golf carts had congregated on earlier.

The blonde smiled. "Selma sent over churros and iced tea for your men in case they need something."

Cole's blood froze. *That voice.* He studied the woman and his heart stumbled inside his chest. Her shapely figure proved she'd grown into a delectably curvy woman as he'd always expected she would, but her face was almost the same, just more refined. "Lacey Winters?"

Her brows furrowed and her button nose wrinkled as she peered back at him. Had he really changed so much in eight years? Yeah, probably. He'd been a bean pole last he'd seen her…the night he broke it off with her.

She gave up trying to figure out who he was. "I'm sorry. Do I know you?"

He should let it go. No need to dredge up the past. He had a fire to control.

His pulse went into overdrive. Another fire. It couldn't be coincidence. He scowled at her. "You should. I'm Cole, Cole Hatcher."

Even in the reflection of the flames, her face turned pasty white and he kicked himself for revealing his identity. All he needed now was a fainting woman to contend with.

"You two know each other?" The other woman leaned on one hip, her concern for Lacey evident in the look she gave him.

At the owner's voice, Lacey recovered her color. Actually, her face changed from white to an angry flush in a matter of seconds. It reminded him of a flashover.

"Not that I want to know him." Lacey handed the tray over to the owner and stepped up to him. She poked her index finger into his chest. Hard. "So, Cole Hatcher. Are you going to accuse me of setting this fire? After all, I'm here, on the same property. It's not like you need evidence or anything. Feel free to assume the worst. I'm sure it helps to justify the way you treated me." She pulled back as if touching him made her feel sick. "Good luck with that." Turning on her heel, she stalked off, her hips swaying enticingly until he remembered where he was and who he was looking at.

"So *you're* the one who broke her heart." The owner studied him briefly then set the tray on the ground and followed after Lacey.

Shit.

Lacey didn't have a destination in mind. She didn't even see the dirt road she walked on. All she could see was Cole Hatcher, or rather the new and improved Cole Hatcher. He'd grown even taller and had filled out like a pro football player. What right did he have to look that good?

"Lacey, wait." Kendra's voice stopped her.

She didn't want to wait. She wanted to get as far from Cole as she could. That was why she'd applied for the job at Poker Flat in the first place. But Kendra was her boss.

"Lacey." Kendra grabbed her arm. "Were you planning to walk into the ravine?"

She looked at her boss blankly before refocusing on her surroundings in the growing darkness. Shoot. She'd almost walked right off the road.

She returned her gaze to Kendra and shook her head, her eyes watering at her near miss. She shouldn't let Cole affect her so much. She was supposed to be over him by now.

Kendra looped her arm in hers. "Come on. Let's let the firefighters do their job and you can tell me all about it."

Lacey swallowed the lump in her throat. "I'd rather not."

"That wasn't a request." Kendra tugged on her arm and she gave in. Her boss was twice her size and tough. Besides, Lacey owed her an explanation. Her broken heart and arson charge had been the two deciding factors for getting hired. Kendra only hired misfits and at first Lacey had appeared too perfect.

She sniffed. Heck, she was anything but perfect.

"So he's the one who broke your heart, isn't he?" Kendra didn't waste time getting to the point.

"Yes."

"I thought you said he was a cowboy and lived in Orson, Arizona."

Lacey pulled up her memory of the young man she'd fallen head over heels for. He'd been six feet tall as a high school senior and as thin as any wrangler, but even then his hard chin had given him a more mature look. Her weakness, though, had been his eyes. Cole Hatcher had always had the kindest green eyes she'd ever gazed into.

"Lacey?"

"Yes, he is, he was, I don't know. I have no idea what he's doing here or why he's a firefighter." Her stomach tensed. The last time they were at a fire together, he held her close as her parents' carriage house went up in smoke.

Kendra steered her toward her own casita. "I think we'd better have this conversation at your place."

Lacey stopped, forcing Kendra to halt. "We can't do that. We have guests and they will all be in the main building asking questions, needing food and attention."

"Of course they will, and Wade and Selma can take care of

them. You and I are going to your casita." Kendra tugged her into walking again.

She sighed. She'd finally forgotten about Cole, except for the dull ache of her bruised heart. She'd moved on, gone to college, done what was right, as she always had…except he'd ignored that fact when he decided to agree with the rest of the town.

Kendra stepped back when they reached the door to her casita.

Pulling her resort keyring from the pocket in her skirt, Lacey quickly identified her house key and unlocked the door. She flicked the light switch and a pale-yellow glow filled the living room. "Would you like some lemonade?"

Kendra hooked her arm again and steered her to her white wicker couch with the cactus floral cushions. "No, I don't want anything to drink. I want you to tell me why you and that hunk of a firefighter out there aren't living happily ever after on a ranch in Orson."

Lacey sat and clasped her hands as Kendra pulled the matching wicker chair over to sit opposite her.

"I'm not sure where to start."

"Okay, then I'll ask the questions and you answer them. How long had you two been an item?"

Technically, they had met sophomore year of high school, but it was their junior year that they became an item. "About two years."

"How long has it been since you last saw him?"

She gripped her hands tighter. "Eight years."

"And what caused the breakup?"

Lacey narrowed her eyes. "That stupid arson charge." Her

tone dripped with bitterness she couldn't control. She'd always been a good girl, and being accused of something she didn't do had rankled.

"Ah, so he broke up with you because he thought you were a firebug and as a future firefighter he couldn't be with you."

"Yes. No. I mean, yes, he did believe the accusations and dumped me because he couldn't be with 'someone like me' as he so graciously put it. But he was a cowboy then, not a firefighter. He was supposed to stay in Orson and take over his parents' horse ranch."

Kendra pondered that information for a moment. "But didn't you say when I hired you that they ruled that fire as accidental?"

She shrugged. "Yes, but by the time they made that decision, I was away at school and my reputation in Orson was dirt." The fact was, she'd been lucky to escape from the burning carriage house. It had taken her over a year to get over the nightmares of waking up in the dark, her lungs filling with smoke.

Kendra stood. "I want you to stay in this casita all night. I don't want anyone trying to blame this fire on you."

"You believe me?"

Her boss rolled her eyes. "Lacey, I didn't have to work with you for a year and let you handle all my money to know you wouldn't have started a fire. The fact that some idiot who supposedly loved you couldn't figure it out doesn't mean the rest of the world is so stupid."

Tears welled in her eyes and Lacey threw her arms around Kendra. "Thank you."

Her boss gave her a tight hug, then pushed her back. "First rule, don't let him see your weakness. Got it?"

Lacey nodded and brushed her tears away with the hem of her western shirt, even though her heart was breaking all over again. Kendra had been a professional poker player and if anyone would know how to appear to Cole, it would be her.

"Second, don't give him the opportunity to point fingers. Go about your daily business as if nothing unusual has happened."

She nodded. "But what about the real reason the fire started?"

Kendra scowled. "Shit, that could be anything from more vandals hating our nudist business to a careless construction worker to a guest with an arson record. We'll let the fire department figure that out. Okay?"

"Okay." She straightened her shoulders. "I'll stay here tonight and review Selma's inventory. I have it on my computer."

Kendra walked to the door. "Good. Maybe you can also check our reservations and see if anyone is due to arrive tomorrow. I'd like to know what kind of guest relation mitigation we will be up against with the police and fire people here."

"Already did." Lacey opened the door for her boss. "No one is due to check in until Wednesday when Ginger and Buddy arrive, unless we have day guests."

Kendra smiled. "Good. That's one thing in our favor. Ginger and Buddy won't care." Instead of turning away, her boss shifted her weight, a clear sign she was concerned.

Lacey's stomach tightened. "What is it?"

"I just realized how important it is for me to hire a new security guard. It's been so quiet this fall I haven't made time for interviews. Now with your ex in the area, I'm thinking that should become my first priority."

She was about to reassure Kendra that Cole didn't have a

dangerous bone in his body, but she swallowed her words as the image of him hefting his fellow firefighters away from the flames came to mind. The teenage Cole certainly didn't have that kind of strength. Truth be told, she didn't know *this* Cole Hatcher at all.

~~~~~

Cole fell into a cushioned chair in the Poker Flat Nudist Resort's lobby and lifted the neck of his t-shirt up to wipe his eyes. The material came away dotted with tiny black specks. Shit, he needed a shower. Just a few more minutes and he could head back to the station.

Wade Johnson, the resort manager, strode away in search of his fiancée, the owner of Poker Flat. The man had stayed up all night with him. Their mutual interest in protecting the horses had Cole thinking. It may be a nudist resort but it was still a resort. He couldn't pass up a possible opportunity for the horses from his and his grandfather's ranch. He'd see if he could get a business card.

Crossing his legs at his ankles, Cole leaned back. He had to admit the resort was first class. The chair he sat in was so comfortable he'd have to be careful not to fall asleep. He glanced at the wooden clock above the receptionist desk. 5:50 a.m. He doubted many nudist guests would be up yet. He could close his eyes until Wade returned. Watching for hot spots all night to protect the desert and the horses had been a strain on the eyes.

A slight change in air temperature was the only warning he had he wasn't alone anymore.

"Oh come on, Selma. You were sitting at your kitchen table twiddling your fingers waiting for the sun to rise. Now you have an extra ten minutes to prep your huevos rancheros."

"Humph. Could have used the extra minutes for my beauty sleep."

Cole opened one eye. Lacey strode toward the front desk in a pair of white cowgirl boots with fringe, a too short white skirt, and a loose white blouse with tiny pink stars and six-shooters printed on it. The only thing missing was a white hat, except she had that too, in her hand. From behind she made him think of a piece of tres leches cake with strawberries on top. The desire to eat her up hit him in the groin.

She stopped at the desk and gave the shorter woman with salt-and-pepper hair a quick hug. "You are far too beautiful as it is."

The woman ducked away, grumbling, but Lacey smiled after her fondly. Cole's heart thumped hard in his chest. He remembered that smile. It had made him believe he could conquer the world. Too bad he hadn't had her with him when he needed to conquer his parents.

Lacey moved to adjust the pamphlets on the side of the counter. Her shapely legs had a slight tan as they disappeared beneath the ass-hugging skirt. He scowled. She shouldn't wear such revealing clothes to work. Was she looking to get laid? Her straight blonde hair was caught in a braid on one side of her neck, giving her an innocent look.

She wasn't innocent at all. As a randy teen, he'd made sure of that. Need slithered through his crotch and up his backbone. The first time he'd had her petite body beneath his own, he'd been afraid of crushing her. But his little lady was made of sterner stuff on the inside. His balls tightened and he shifted in the chair, his erection making him uncomfortable. She'd been so tight.

"What are *you* doing here?"

CHAPTER TWO

She must have heard the creak of the chair when he moved. Shit. She faced him now from across the room, her stance rigid.

Leaning forward, resting his elbows on his knees to hide his hard-on, he tried for a nonchalant attitude. He didn't need her to know his body remembered hers. "I never left. There was a fire last night. Remember?"

Her face softened. "You all worked through the night?"

He shook his head as much to answer her as at the obvious concern in her voice. "No. I sent the men with the tanker back to the station. Only myself and Mason stayed with the engine to be sure the fire was completely out."

She dropped her hat on the desk and sighed. "I better tell Selma. She'll want to get you breakfast." Her tone made it clear she wasn't happy about that. She walked toward the main room, but he didn't want her to leave.

"No. That's okay." He stood. "We're heading back to the station now. I'm just waiting for Wade to find Kendra."

She hesitated before clasping her hands in front of her and leaning against one of the wood post supports. "If you're waiting for Kendra, it will be awhile. She's a night owl and I doubt she got much sleep at all last night. It will take Wade some time to wake her at this hour."

"That's fine. Mason and I will eat when we get back to the station."

"Okay." She stood staring at him but not meeting his gaze.

The silence became awkward. Hell. They were two adults now. Their relationship had ended a long time ago. Certainly they could have a civil conversation. "Why are you working here, at a nudist resort?"

Her gaze flew to his and she stood straighter. "You mean how could I stoop so low as to work here? As a matter of fact, after getting my degree in accounting and graduating summa cum laude, I had my pick of jobs, but I chose to work here because these are good people, and there's absolutely nothing wrong with being nude." She put one hand on her hip and narrowed her eyes. "In fact, I remember a few times when you were wont to prance around in the buff."

Heat rushed to his cheeks. Yeah, as a dumbass adolescent, he may have pulled a couple pranks. But he wasn't a teenager anymore. "I never pranced."

She brushed his comment aside. "Whatever."

No, not whatever. "I was a teenager then. What's your excuse?"

"I don't need an excuse. It's exactly your kind of people who judge nudists that is enough for me to want to help."

He stiffened at the image of Lacey without clothes filling his mind. "You don't actually walk around nude, do you?"

"What if I do? What's it to you?" Her chin came up in challenge.

Shit. Just the thought of her parading around the resort absolutely naked had his heartbeat racing and his cock growing hard. She had filled out so nicely he could imagine what she might look like, but now he wanted to know for sure.

Footsteps approaching from the large room to the right saved him from saying something he would regret.

Kendra Lowe walked in and stopped in front of him, not seeing Lacey. "Wade said you needed to talk to me?"

"Yes, ma'am. The fire is now completely out. Later today you'll receive a visit from an investigator. He needs to determine why the fire started. Don't let the construction crew touch anything. They'll probably want to know what of theirs was damaged. If they get here before the investigator, keep them on this side of the resort or tell them to come back tomorrow."

The woman cocked her head. "Very well. I hope the investigation won't take long. I'd rather my guests not be disturbed too much. As it is, I will have to discount their stay."

"Hopefully it won't, but you have to let the investigator determine the cause of the fire. I'm assuming you had insurance on the new construction?"

"Of course."

Cole grabbed the paperwork he'd left on the side table next to the chair he'd relaxed in for those brief moments. "I'll need you to fill out this sheet and then we'll be on our way."

Kendra took the paper. "Let me get a pen." She turned and walked toward the front desk.

He followed, scanning the area behind it for Lacey, but she

wasn't there. He ignored his disappointment and focused on the owner. She took a pen from behind the counter and filled in the information needed.

The door behind him opened and he turned to see if it was Wade. He wanted to get the man's contact information. But the couple entering the building was definitely not the resort manager. In fact, they were both naked except for flip-flops and they carried a bag and towels.

Kendra glanced up. "Can I help you?"

The young woman, no older than Lacey, had naturally red hair on her head and at the juncture of her thighs, as well as a smattering of freckles on her cheeks. "Yes, we drove up from Phoenix to try Poker Flat for the day. I know it's way early, but we wanted to get the most for our grounds fees." She gave an apologetic smile.

Kendra nodded. "That's a smart idea. One moment." The owner disappeared down the narrow hallway that must lead to the back offices.

The young woman turned her attention to him. "Are you here for the day as well?"

He swallowed, making a conscious effort to look only at her face and not at her very large nipples. He was well aware she was with her man. "No, miss. I was just about to leave."

"Hey, are you a firefighter? Is there a fire?" The young man craned his neck to look past his girl and out the floor-to-ceiling windows of the lobby.

Cole took a tired breath. "No need to worry. The fire is out and no one was hurt. It shouldn't interfere with your day."

The young lady gave an exaggerated sigh. "I'm so glad. This is our first time at this particular resort. We'd heard it was beautiful and we're so excited to spend the day checking it out."

He nodded, trying not to smirk. Despite his need for a shower and sleep, he found it amusing that people paid to walk around nude in a public setting.

"May I help you?" Lacey's voice came from behind the front desk, pulling his attention to her.

She focused solely on the young couple and ignored his presence. He wished he could do the same. She looked so much like his old Lacey but different. Did she still wear the scent that reminded him of clean sheets drying on an outdoor line? Did she still wear the fancy panties and bras she'd been so fond of as a teenager? His nickname for her when they were alone had been Racy Lacey.

He couldn't help staring at her chest as she helped the guests, trying to see through the white blouse to identify any lace or polka dots.

Kendra returned. "I'm sorry about that. I had to find the insurance company's number."

He nodded absently as she continued to fill out the form. He tried to stay focused, but Lacey's welcoming voice had him glancing her way again.

She smiled warmly as she handed the couple a map. "When you are ready to leave, just let any of the staff know and they will call Billy to take you back to your car. Enjoy your day."

When the young couple turned to leave, Lacey spared him a glance. It was anything but friendly.

Maybe he was punchy from lack of sleep, but he smiled in response. She was still damn beautiful, her light-brown eyes matching the mahogany-stained beams of the lobby.

Those eyes widened before she spun on her heel and disappeared again.

He turned back to the owner of Poker Flat to find her studying him. Shit. She knew all about his past with Lacey.

"Here you go."

"Thank you, ma'am. Mason and I are heading out now, but expect the investigator this morning." He turned to leave, but Kendra put her hand on his arm. "Cole."

He started at the use of his name. She'd only called him Lieutenant until now. "Yes?"

"Lacey didn't do it. This one or the last one. You might want to chew on that."

Before he could respond, Kendra Lowe strode back the way she'd come. Shaking his head at her message, he chalked it up to loyalty among women and headed out the door.

Jumping into the engine truck, he sat back as Mason drove them off the nudist resort. No matter what the owner believed, he had an obligation to let Detective Sean Anderson know what he knew. Lacey Winters had been accused of arson once before.

Lacey contemplated the coffee cup in her hands. The dark-brown color reminded her of Cole's hair when they were younger. Now his hair was cut very short. Did he do that for his role as firefighter?

Kendra poked her head around the corner. "All clear. You can go back out to the front desk. He's gone."

"I was just having some coffee." She held up her cup. "Didn't want to drink it in front of check-ins."

"Yeah, right. Since I'm up so damn early, I'm going to the

stable to see if I can coax Wade into a short ride." Kendra paused. "Did you stay up all night working?"

Not exactly. Her nightmare had come back with a vengeance and made her afraid to go back to sleep. She shrugged. "I admit I didn't get a lot of sleep, but I wasn't working."

Kendra gave her a knowing look, probably assuming she'd been thinking about Cole, which in a tangental way she had been.

"Well, stay awake until I get back, okay? You're in charge."

She nodded. "Okay. Have fun."

Kendra left the doorway only to poke her head around it again. "I almost forgot. Price Construction will probably show up soon. Cole said they aren't allowed on the stable ridge until the fire investigator arrives which will be later today. I'll have Wade block the stable road with the wagon so they come directly here. Let them know what happened."

"Got it. And if we have more day guests, they can wait to use that part of the resort until later."

Kendra nodded in agreement then disappeared again, this time for good.

Lacey topped off her coffee and moved to the reception area. She was a wimp for hiding in the back, but she didn't know how to react around Cole. He was the same person but so different physically. He must have added at least fifty pounds of pure muscle since high school.

She set her coffee down and powered-on the computer. In the light of the lobby, she'd been made aware of exactly how big Cole had become. He had to be at least a foot taller than her now and the navy-blue fire department t-shirt fit him like a second skin, showing a broad, mounded chest, narrowed waist and biceps that stretched the short sleeves to their limits. The firefighter pants he wore hid his legs, which just had her imagination running wild. Then he'd had to go and smile at her, his warm green eyes twinkling as if he knew it would make her melt inside.

Shaking her head, she tried to dispel her thoughts of Cole. She sat and reviewed emails from the website asking for information. She always liked to do those first in the hopes of turning them into reservations. She completed three before her mind reverted back to Cole like a quail to her nest. Cole Hatcher's opinion was like a steel trap. Once set, it never changed. Yes, he was charming and courteous and had a good heart, but if she was a *persona non grata* then there was no reason to hope he'd changed his opinion about her over the years. Stubborn cowboy.

She took a sip of her cooling coffee. Cole would probably never set foot on Poker Flat again, so there was no reason for her to worry about him anymore. If anything, seeing him again had helped. In her heart, she'd kept that little flame of love alive all these years, but there was no hope there. She'd been a silly school girl. Now she was a grown woman. She would find a nice man to marry someday. One who would listen to reason and stand by his woman *no matter what.*

That's what she wanted. Loyalty and unending faith. Two qualities she'd not had with Cole.

Feeling a bit more balanced since seeing her ex, she answered a few more emails and then stepped to the back to warm her coffee. When she returned, the front door opened and two men walked in.

Keith, the owner of Price Construction, stalked forward with a scowl, his bald head reflecting the lobby's recessed ceiling lights.

Behind him was John Lockhart, one of the men who worked for Mr. Price. Reflexively, she brushed down her skirt. John was attractive in a rugged way. They'd been flirting a bit when she'd taken Selma's treats out to the site, a job she'd volunteered for after meeting him. Maybe she should ask him out to help her forget about Cole.

"What the hell is going on?" Keith punctuated his question with a meaty fist to the counter. "There's a wagon blocking the road up to the site."

"Good morning, Mr. Price. I'm afraid we've had to halt construction for a while."

"Halt construction? I'm on a deadline thanks to that tight contract Kendra negotiated, and it looked from the ledge top that there's been some kind of damage done. I'll need time to fix that. I can't afford to 'wait a while.'"

Lacey kept her smile. Her mom always said a person could attract more bees with honey than vinegar, even if it wasn't honey the bees were after. "Oh, I'm sure Kendra will renegotiate." She winked. "I'm even guessing it will be more to your benefit." She glanced at John, who was smiling at her. At least her heart didn't race when he looked at her.

Mr. Price slapped his hand on the counter to gain her attention. "Out with it, girl. What are you trying to say?"

"I'm saying there was a fire at the construction site last night."

"What?" Mr. Price looked stunned.

John put his hand on the counter as if he wanted to touch her. "Are you okay? Was anyone hurt?"

"I'm fine, thank you for asking." She smiled at him before turning her attention back to Mr. Price. "No one was hurt but there were four explosions and all the new construction is burnt. Even the old barn boards Kendra had shipped in. So my guess is you will have to start all over again, which will mean more money, right?"

Mr. Price finally relaxed. "Yes, it will. And this time, I'll negotiate a better timeline."

"So why can't we get to the construction site?" John frowned. "Is there anything dangerous there?"

He really did have a great jaw and his wavy blond hair was attractive in a relaxed way. "I don't think there's anything dangerous, but I haven't been there since last night. The firefighters said no one could go to the site until the investigator came to look it all over."

Mr. Price groaned. "This could take forever. I'm going to pull my men to another job. Tell Kendra to call me when she wants to renegotiate and have us start again. If she needs someone to clean up after the investigation is over, I've got a crew for that too."

"Really?" She raised her brows then winked at John.

The older man shifted his weight. "Well, yeah. We have to clean up our sites when we're done, so I use that crew to do odd clean up jobs. Can't hurt to bring in some more money. Not a ton of building going on out this way."

She nodded. Phoenix and more populated areas had recovered from the housing slump, but the smaller towns were still struggling. "I'll be sure to give Kendra the message."

Mr. Price nodded then headed for the exit. John reached out. "I look forward to coming back to work on the project."

She smiled and shook his hand. "I hope it won't be long."

He gave her hand an extra squeeze then followed his boss out. Lacey watched his stride, which was so different from a cowboy's.

Maybe she should keep her sights on men who weren't cowboys. Her luck with them hadn't been so great.

~~~~~

Cole called himself a fool from here 'til Tuesday. What the hell was he doing? "Thanks for letting me tag along, Sean."

The detective with bright-orange hair cut short looked like a young recruit, even after ten years on the force, but Cole knew better. Sean was good at investigation and he'd specifically gone to arson school to be better equipped to help out the fire stations in the area. Cole trusted him to discover the truth.

"I don't mind the company. I also appreciate the information you gave me. It's good to know, but I'll let the evidence lead me to the cause."

"Of course." Cole shrugged as if the outcome of the investigation didn't matter to him. But it did…a lot. "I'm wired after the battle last night. I won't be able to sleep until tonight now. Besides, I'd like to check out what this nudist resort is all about." He didn't want to divulge his interest in setting something up with the resort manager.

Sean took his eyes off the road for a moment to give him a sideways look. "Really?"

Shit, now the man was going to think him a pervert. "Oh, I have no plans to get nude, but I'm curious as to how they operate. I hear they have naked horseback riding. I just don't get that. You could hurt some pretty sensitive parts doing that, if you know what I mean."

Sean grimaced even as he turned down the dirt road with

the new wooden sign declaring the entrance to Poker Flat Nudist Resort. "I don't see anything but desert out here."

Cole grinned. "Wait until after we park. It's well hidden, which is probably a good thing."

They continued down the flat dirt road passing nothing but saguaro, mesquite trees and an occasional ocotillo. Finally, they came to the roadblock, the tire tracks from his fire trucks still visible going around the wooden barrier.

"Pull in here. They'll bring us down in a golf cart." He pointed to the three-sided garage the size of two fire stations.

Sean raised a brow, but didn't comment as he parked the unmarked vehicle in the shade of the giant steel structure. As they exited the car, an older man approached dressed in jeans, a checkered shirt, and suspenders with a rumpled cowboy hat in his hand.

"Welcome to Poker Flat Nudist Resort. I'm Billy." He clutched his hat with one hand and held out the other.

Sean shook. "Detective Sean Anderson. You probably remember Lt. Cole Hatcher from last night."

Billy scrunched up his face as he peered at Cole, and thrust his hand forward. "I were asleep last night. Nice to meet ya."

Cole looked down at the short elderly man and shook his hand. He'd slept through fire engine sirens and gas explosions?

"This way." As Billy led them to a golf cart, Cole studied him a bit closer. Maybe the man was hard of hearing. One way to find out.

Sean sat in the front, so Cole took the back seat. Once they started off toward the edge of the ravine, he quietly commented on the resort, lifting his voice to just above a whisper. "It amazes me how hidden this place is."

Billy turned his head slightly. "I loves that guests is so surprised. I never gets tired of that."

So much for hard of hearing. Maybe the old man had been off the resort when he wasn't supposed to be.

Sean turned toward Cole. "There *is* a resort here, right? This isn't a joke."

Billy chuckled as he slowed the cart at the ridge of the ravine. "There she be."

"Holy sh—cow." Sean stared.

Cole could sympathize with the man. When the fire engine had crested the ravine at sunset yesterday, he'd had a similar reaction, though not so polite. His men had echoed his expletives. From the desert road, the ravine wasn't even noticeable, but once cresting it, the resort came into view, perched high on two large shelves of land on the opposite ravine wall, yet below the top ridge.

One side held the stables, a steel building and the burned construction, while the other shelf held the main building and pool with adobe casitas lined up behind it. More casitas were scattered farther down the sloping wall of the ravine with golf carts parked outside. Between them and the resort was a dirt road with a sturdy bridge at the bottom that crossed the stream, which barely trickled at this time of year.

He pointed at the shelf with the stable. "That's where the fire was."

Billy picked up speed again. While Sean viewed the entire resort, Cole focused on the building in ashes. Its proximity to the barn from this angle made his gut clench. Last night was too close for the horses here.

After crossing the bridge, they rose up the other side of the ravine and at the split, headed left toward the stables.

"Ms. Kendra say you be coming and to keep everyone away. Lacey send the construction guys a packin." Billy smiled a toothy grin, showing a significant gap between his tarnished teeth.

Sean nodded. "Good. What's that?"

Billy slowed the cart. "Sheet, I forget. Wade block the road with the buckboard to keeps everyone away." He brought the cart to a stop.

Cole stepped out. "Can we move it?"

"I doesn't know. Wade use the big horses to pulls this." Billy scratched his head. "I guesses I can walks to the barn and gets Wade."

Sean exited the golf cart and walked around the wagon. "This is a pretty sturdy reproduction piece."

Cole joined him. "I think we can move this. You two guide it at the front and I'll push from behind. We only need to move it far enough for the golf cart to get by."

"It can't hurt to try." Sean patted Billy on the shoulder. "Come on, Billy. Time for your morning workout."

Billy grumbled something unintelligible and Cole smiled. He doubted very much that Billy was excited, but if this worked, it would save them at least a half hour.

He strode behind the replica of an old western wagon, glad he wore his Stetson because the morning heat was well on its way to the low nineties. He leaned against the wagon to test its willingness to move. Though it had four sturdy wooden wheels, it didn't even rock. Not a good sign.

"Ready when you are, Cole." Sean looked back at him from the horse hitch.

Pressing his hands against the back of the wagon's bed, he pushed. The wagon rocked but remained in place. Shit.

Sean yelled back, "Need some help?"

He shook his head. "And get your pretty clothes dirty?"

"Trust me. They'll be dirty soon enough."

Cole grinned. Investigating fires wasn't exactly clean work. "Let me give it another try. I just need to get it rolling."

He didn't wait for a response. Instead, he leaned his back against the wagon and used his leg muscles. The vehicle rocked, creaked, and finally rolled. Not wanting to lose the momentum, he quickly shuffled his feet back and pushed harder. When the wagon had rolled a good fifteen feet, he stopped. He turned to see where they had directed it. Billy and Sean had angled the wagon so the horses could easily be hitched. He was glad someone was thinking.

Sean walked over. "You guys obviously don't have enough fires to go to. It looks like you spend your shifts working out on the equipment at the station."

He shrugged. "Hey, it was donated to us. The least we can do is use it between calls."

"I may just start coming by once a week." He patted his lean stomach. "Detective work isn't helping my beer belly."

Cole raised one eyebrow. "Yeah, right."

Billy drove the golf cart to where they stood. "Ready?"

They both resumed their seats and Billy headed up to the burn site. When they arrived, they climbed out.

Sean immediately switched into detective mode. "Billy, thank you. We will find you when we need a ride back."

"Okay." The old man smiled then headed the golf cart toward the barn.

Cole tamped down his interest in the barn and focused on the wet debris spread over thirty yards. What was the building going to be? The layout gave no clue.

"Explain to me where the fire was when you arrived." Sean took out a pad of paper and a pen. "Then walk me through your strategy for knocking it down."

Cole filled Sean in on the entire night from driving up to the blaze, the explosions, the old barn wood, the precautionary measures and the decision to let it go. The man took copious notes on his pad.

"And you say the woman you knew from another fire was here?"

"Yes. She brought out churros and iced tea for the men."

Sean raised his brows. "Really? I like this place already."

He kept his thoughts to himself. He'd been pissed when he'd seen her walking up with food, but he and his men had devoured it shortly after, as well as the sandwiches Kendra brought them later in the night when it was only himself and Mason.

"So tell me about the other fire this woman was accused of starting."

Cole's gut tightened. He didn't want this fire to be laid at Lacey's door, but he had to tell Sean what he knew. "Lacey Winters is her name. Eight years ago she used to hang out in an old carriage house on her parents' property. It was her space to gather with friends of which I was one. One night a friend called me to tell me the carriage house was on fire. I rushed over and Lacey had soot on her clothes." He didn't need to tell Sean it was Lacey who called him. The less the detective knew about their past relationship, the better.

He never forgot how her hair smelled like smoke as he held

her in his arms while they watched the building burn to the ground. The firefighters had focused on protecting the barn and the house, very much like he'd done last night.

"How did the arson charge come about?"

He shrugged. "I'm not sure. I wasn't privy to the investigation. I was just a senior in high school at the time, but rumors were rampant. The next thing we all hear, she's been charged with arson and then later the charges were dropped. I do know there was gasoline involved as there were two explosions at that fire."

"What was the carriage house used for?"

"Mostly storage." He envisioned the place as it was when he hung out there with Lacey. They enjoyed not only the old couch, but the old bean bag chair, the saw horses, the antique rocker and the gilt-framed mirror. "There were antiques in there as well as old junk, like family portraits, clothes, and old toys."

Sean scribbled on his pad. "So no reason for gasoline to be in there?"

"Actually, there were also old farm tools, a weed whacker, lawn mower and stuff. It kind of doubled as a garage, I guess."

More scribbling. "Okay, got it. Now I need to get to work on this one. I'll let you know when I'm ready to leave."

Cole took the hint. "Good luck."

Sean shook his head. "I don't need luck. I just need to read the story written in this debris."

He nodded. His own goal was to make captain so he could go to arson investigation training. The extra cash couldn't hurt. He didn't want his grandparents to have to help support his horse project forever.

With that project in mind, he strode toward the state-of-the-art barn in hopes of catching Wade inside. He'd learned last night that the stable manager was on vacation for two weeks, so Wade was the person he needed to convince. Billy's golf cart was gone. He must have returned to the garage to wait for other visitors.

As Cole stepped into the relatively cool shade of the red structure, he noticed two horses had recently been brought in for a good combing. That meant whoever was planning to do the work should be back shortly.

He took the opportunity to walk by the stalls. Including the two horses in the grooming area, there were four others, but another ten stalls remained empty. The first six had name placards for each horse. His heart beat harder at the potential. If the resort did a good business, they would need more horses...maybe his horses. Opening the barn doors at the back, he found a large empty corral. The place could be the perfect home for his rescues, if they were treated well.

"Can I help you?" He recognized the male voice before he turned around.

"Yes, Wade. You may just be able to." He strode forward then tipped his hat toward Kendra. "Ma'am."

She looked at him quizzically before recognition dawned. "Oh, it's Cole." Her eyes narrowed. "What are you doing here?"

He forcibly kept himself from shuffling his feet beneath her hard stare. "I'm not here on official business. Just wanted to talk horses with Wade here, if that's okay, unless of course I should be talking to you."

Her demeanor changed from affronted to uninterested in seconds. She waved her hand. "If it's horse talk, you can chat with him. I have to get back to my office." She put her hand on Wade's. "Thanks for the ride."

Wade smirked and wiggled his brows. "Anytime."

The two had obviously gone for a ride, and from the looks of it, had sex out in the desert. Talk about uncomfortable.

Kendra winked and sauntered out the open barn doors. Cole opened his mouth to ask about the trails, when Kendra came back in. "Who moved the wagon?" She didn't sound happy.

Cole suddenly felt as if he'd done something wrong. "I did, ma'am. We needed to get the golf cart by so the investigator could reach the burn site."

The woman stared at him as if he'd turned into a jackrabbit. Then she raised her brows at Wade.

The man shook his head, his smirk firmly in place. "That's one heavy wagon to be moving without draft horses."

"Yeah, tell me about it." Cole rolled his shoulders.

Kendra turned back to him. "When you're done talking horses, maybe you could help Wade hook up the team and move the wagon back to the barn."

"Yes, ma'am."

Wade opened his mouth, but Kendra spoke. "Don't call me 'ma'am'. Kendra will do."

He nodded, keeping his mouth shut. It was too much a habit to risk saying it again, so he kept quiet. Luckily, she didn't wait for a reply and left.

"What can I help you with?" Wade strolled over to the two horses waiting to be attended to.

Cole followed him, noticing the Arabians were particularly fine horses. He had an Arabian on the ranch. Elsa was well built, but scars marred her neck, making it look like the hair of her mane was falling out. "These are good-looking horses."

Wade began to rub one of them down. "This is Ace and that one is Sundancer. I got them from the same ranch."

"Do you always buy your horses in pairs?"

Wade stopped and looked at him. "So far, but not for any particular reason. Why?"

Cole had pitched his horses many times and been shot down more times than he could count. He steeled himself for rejection again. "I have a number of horses for sale, but none are matching pairs."

Wade resumed rubbing down Ace. "I'm always on the lookout for new horses, but they need to be dead broke because these riders are completely inexperienced."

"That makes sense. I have a number that would fit that category." Mainly because they were almost dead when he'd obtained them. Others, though, were far too afraid of humans. Those he would never be able to sell.

"Do you have a website?" Wade didn't pause in his chore. "I usually research online before taking a drive to who knows where. I got these two from a little town near Payson."

Cole hesitated. His horses didn't show well, which is why he never put full body shots on his site and the few photos up there were to add to the general write up about Last Chance Ranch. "I have a site, but my horses aren't up there. I'm just outside Wickenburg on the west side if you'd like to come by."

Wade dropped the curry comb on a nearby table and looked over the two horses to stare him in the eye. "Why wouldn't you have photos of your horses on your site?"

No more beating around the bush. "Because they don't look as pretty as what you have here. My horses are rescues. When horses have been abused, starved, abandoned or have an injury an owner can't afford to fix and is going to put them down, I take them. Once I have nursed them back to health, I sell them to resorts who are willing to have less than perfect horses for their guests to ride."

Wade stared at him for a couple moments, then laughed.

CHAPTER THREE

Cole fisted his hands. He'd had people shake their heads, but never had someone laugh at him. What he did was not a laughing matter. Some of the horses he saved had turned his stomach when he'd first seen them.

"I'm sorry." Wade smiled and stepped around the Arabians. "I'm not laughing at you. I'm laughing at Kendra and her unique ability to attract those who need a second chance. I only thought she attracted people, but it sounds like she attracts animals too now."

He had no idea what the man was talking about, but he relaxed his stance. "So you might be interested?"

Wade clapped him on the shoulder. "I'm not just interested. I think once Kendra finds out, she won't let me order a horse from anywhere else."

Cole breathed deeply. To have this new resort buying his horses could be the boost they needed. "Like I said, they're not perfect."

Wade grinned. "That's even better."

"I don't understand."

Wade slipped his hand into the curry comb and moved around Ace to start on the horse's other side. "Kendra doesn't hire anyone who doesn't need a second chance. You met Billy." Cole nodded. "He was a homeless drunk when Kendra hired him."

Cole hadn't smelled any alcohol on the man, but then again it looked like he'd just come from a shower.

"And you tasted Selma's cooking last night, right?"

"Yes. The churros were excellent and the sandwich had a great mix of flavors. Why?" Hopefully, the cook hadn't been up on murder charges…for poisoning.

"She'd just closed her brothel when Kendra hired her."

Cole started to get the picture. So why would Kendra hire Lacey? She was perfect, even more so now. He looked at Wade and found the man staring at him.

"Lacey was hired because of her broken heart."

Cole swallowed hard as his own heart constricted. He'd done the right thing back in high school, but it still hurt. He had always felt something for her. Hell, he'd felt a lot for her. Every girlfriend he'd had since had been compared to Lacey.

"That and the arson charge." Wade returned to his chore.

Cole started. "The arson charge was dropped." He'd still been in Orson when the county sheriff had ruled the fire accidental. But by then, Lacey had gone off to college.

Wade shrugged. "The fact she'd been accused and run out of town was enough for Kendra."

"She wasn't run out of town."

Wade raised one eyebrow. "Maybe not literally, but by her

account, she'd become a pariah." The man's face turned stern. "But she's family here and we stick by our family."

Cole got the message loud and clear. He was the outsider on Poker Flat so he better not cause any trouble. He didn't plan on it. He did his duty by telling Sean about Lacey's past and he hoped to sell a couple horses. "And why did Kendra hire you?"

Wade grinned. "She wouldn't have if she'd had a choice, but she'd been desperate for a stable manager. She said I was too 'perfect'. Luckily for me, she proved what an ass I could be, but gave me a second chance anyway."

There was obviously a lot more to that story, but he wasn't there to get involved in the past escapades of the Poker Flat staff. He was there to sell horses. "It sounds like my horses would fit in here. Do the guests really ride naked?"

Wade finished with Ace and moved to Sundancer. "Yeah, they do. We keep the horses at a walk and use special covers over the saddles. Even so, they always bring their own towels to sit on. The guests really enjoy it." He paused. "There's nothing like seeing the joy in a person's eyes the first time they ride a horse. You know what I mean?"

"Yes, I do." He'd never forget the day he'd first convinced Lacey to get up on a horse. Her parents owned a cattle ranch and despite the cowboys riding horses, no one had ever asked her if she'd like to ride. She'd actually been afraid of them.

He'd had to bribe her to just sit on his horse, Thunder. When he finally handed her up there, she looked petrified. He walked the horse around the corral and she slowly relaxed until she was absolutely beaming, her bright smile making her shine. When she'd finally come down and into his arms, she told him she loved him for the first time.

"Hey, cowboy, you still with me?" Wade's voice snapped him from his memory.

"Sure."

"I said, do you want to help me get Sage and Daisy hooked up to the wagon?"

He smiled. "I better. I promised Kendra I would and I have a feeling she'd be none too pleased if I reneged."

Wade walked Ace out back and let him loose in the corral. "You've got that right." Wade pointed to the last stall with a name placard. "That's Daisy. You can bring her and I'll get Sage as soon as I move Sundancer."

Cole walked up to the stall and Daisy stepped up to meet him. She was a beautiful Belgian with good bone structure. As the horse pushed her head against his shoulder, he grinned. Reaching into his pocket, he pulled out a small bag of jelly beans, poured a few into his hand and gave them to her. He'd forgotten to take them out of his jeans after giving Elsa her favorite treat this morning. "You have a good nose, sweetie."

Wade walked by with Sundancer in tow. "Watch her. She does like t-shirts."

"Thanks for the warning." He ducked to the side as Daisy pulled back her lips to grasp his shirt in her teeth. "I don't think so, girl. Come on."

He walked her slowly toward the wagon, his eyes scanning the other half of the resort. Was Lacey still at the front desk? Is that what she did here? She'd always been good with numbers, even tutoring him in math.

He looked back to see Wade leading Sage. He'd try to nail the man down as far as a date to come out to the ranch. He hadn't sold a horse in over four months and while his firefighter salary and small investments could keep the ranch going if he only had ten horses, he currently had thirteen and there were a couple pretty big vet bills coming in.

Movement in his peripheral vision had him turning his head. Sean was completely engrossed in his work, walking through the debris, taking pictures and scribbling notes. It might be a while before Cole could leave. He returned his gaze to the other half of the resort. It had to be lunchtime by now. He wouldn't mind another one of Poker Flat's sandwiches…or a chance to see Lacey again.

~~~~~

"You're all set, Mrs. Landry. I have you down for two for the sunset trail ride. Be sure to be at the barn by five."

Lacey closed the trail ride reservation screen as the day guest smiled happily up at her husband before the two walked hand in hand toward the lobby doors. Before they reached them, a man with clothes entered. That caught her attention as only staff wore clothes, unless it was a newbie nudist. Most nudists shucked their clothes the minute they parked their car in the garage on the other side of the ravine.

The man smiled warmly at her and it took her a moment to recognize him. "John?"

"You bet." He leaned his elbow on the front counter, which showed his bulging forearm and biceps. He was dressed in a sleeveless t-shirt that read "Sturgis 2014" and a pair of black jeans and biker boots.

As a woman, she definitely appreciated the view of his arms. "What are you doing here?"

He shrugged. "Well, the boss didn't need me at the other site, so I have the day off and I thought it might be a great opportunity to have lunch with you. You do get to take a lunch, don't you?"

Though she usually ate at the front counter, the concern he revealed that he might be wrong had her changing her plans. "Of course I do. Just let me get someone to cover for me. I'll be right back."

She hurried through the back hallway, touched that John had come all the way back to Poker Flat to have lunch with her. He seemed like a nice man and this was the perfect opportunity to learn more about him. At least he already knew she worked at a nudist resort. She'd only been on two dates since the resort opened. One man had been appalled she worked at Poker Flat, while the other practically salivated in his attempt to obtain a free day pass.

She poked her head into her boss's office. "Kendra?"

Kendra didn't look up from her paperwork. "Hmmm?"

"Could you cover the front desk so I can eat lunch in the dining room?"

"Why?" Kendra glanced up. She didn't show her curiosity, but it was very much in her tone.

"John Lockhart came back to ask me to lunch."

"Really?" A slow smirk grew on Kendra's face. She was still getting used to showing her emotions and the knowing smile was a new one. "I'd be happy to. I can read this insurance policy anywhere. Go ahead, I'll handle the front."

"Thank you." Lacey headed down the hall, but made a quick trip into the bathroom to redo her braid. When she entered the lobby, she gave John a smile. "All set."

"Great." He held out his bulky arm and she took it. She

wasn't used to this side of him. When she'd been the one to go to the construction site to bring iced tea and Selma's latest snack, he was dressed in a grungy t-shirt, usually soaked through with perspiration and stubble lining his chin, but he was always quick to smile. His blond hair was a little long and by mid-afternoon pasted to his brow with sweat. His nose was a bit large for his face, but his blue eyes reminded her of Santa Claus. That and he did have a little bit of a belly.

As they walked into the dining room, she felt a certain pride that he cleaned up so well. Selma stopped mid-stride, her brown eyes widening, before she continued through the batwing doors to the kitchen, the bun in her black hair bouncing with her step. Rachel, a young woman who had been caught stealing from her last employer, showed them to a table. Since all expenses were paid upon checkout, there was little to tempt Rachel at Poker Flat. The pretty redheaded waitress wiggled her brows at Lacey behind John's back.

They took their seats across from each other and ordered drinks. Her instinct told her John would have liked a beer, but he kept it to iced tea.

"I'm sorry we didn't have a chance to call Mr. Price before he and the crew came out this morning. There was just so much going on."

John shook his head. "He'll get over it, especially once we start working on the building again. Truth be told, it's a godsend. It means a whole new contract and new money. I know he's been struggling financially. Last month, he even took a small job out in Cave Creek."

She raised her glass. "Here's to the silver lining on unfortunate events. Mr. Price will have another job and I get to have lunch with you."

As they clinked their glasses, he grinned. He really did have a great smile.

Someone walked by her then stopped next to John. "Hi, Lacey."

She looked up and her breath caught in her throat even as her heart started to patter like a Gila woodpecker on a saguaro cactus. Cole Hatcher, in snug blue jeans, a t-shirt that looked like it'd been melted against him and his cowboy hat in hand, stood facing her. Staring up into his eyes, she couldn't help but compare him to her lunch date. Both men were muscular but Cole was less bulky and more defined. He was definitely taller, and there was no denying his straight nose and strong chin caused her throat to go dry. She took a quick sip of tea. "Cole, what are you still doing here?"

"I haven't been here all morning. I just hitched a ride back with Detective Anderson."

She frowned. "Why? You want to make sure the right person is accused of setting the fire?"

He held his hands up in front of him. "Whoa. I'm just here to talk to Wade about buying a few horses."

"Horses? I thought you were a firefighter now."

"I am, but since I don't breed horses, I need to support them somehow."

What was he talking about? "Can't your parents support them?"

"No." He frowned and anger crept into his voice. "They don't have a use for my horses. That's why mine are at my grandparents' ranch outside of Wickenburg."

Oh sugar, she'd forgotten his grandparents owned a spread out there.

John stood and offered his hand. "Hi, I'm John Lockhart."

"Cole Hatcher." He shook hands with John but returned his gaze to her. "I don't want to disturb your lunch." He gave a quick nod. "Lacey." He strode away, taking a seat at a table behind her. Good. That way she wouldn't have to look at him while having lunch with John.

John watched Cole move off before returning his attention to her. "I take it he was one of the firefighters from last night. Guess you've known him a while."

She tried to focus on what John was saying but her stupid heart wouldn't slow down. "He's my ex."

"Ex-husband?" John stiffened.

"No, an ex-boyfriend from a long time ago."

"Hmmm." John took a sip of his iced tea and studied the menu.

Lacey couldn't let the comment go. "Hmmm, what?"

He looked up at her. "I'd say, by the way he's staring over here, he isn't happy about being an ex."

Really? "He dumped me back in high school and you can imagine how long ago that was, so I think if he's staring over here he's probably just wondering about what you could possibly see in me." She forced a laugh.

Cole was staring at them? Maybe he was trying to figure out if they had started the fire together.

"I can't believe anyone would dump you." John reached across the table and put his hand on hers.

His touch was strange, but comforting. At least John liked her, though he really didn't know her. "Thank you. Let's forget about him. What are you going to have? You do know everything Selma makes is excellent, right?"

He grinned. "I can definitely vouch for her snacks. I can't wait to try her lunch."

As they ordered and waited for their meals, Lacey did well to focus on John, but when her meal arrived and she bit into the fish taco she'd ordered, it reminded her of the first time she and Cole tried fish tacos at a little cantina in the middle of nowhere when they were delivering one of his dad's horses. She hadn't thought about that in years.

They had actually dared each other to try one. A lot of betting ensued with her losing, though she'd won in the end as the loser had to be on the bottom. She flushed at the memory and quickly gulped down more iced tea.

"Lacey, are you okay?" John's concern caused guilt to rise. She needed to focus on him.

She touched her chest with her free hand. "Don't worry about me. Sometimes the spices Selma uses can be a little hot for me."

He looked at his taco then straightened a little. "This tastes pretty mild to me. Guess you're a lightweight."

She nodded and took another bite, ashamed she'd been thinking of Cole while having lunch with John. "Do you do any cooking?"

John grimaced. "Not if I can help it. Sure I can make a pretty mean sandwich and I can grill burgers with the best of them, but I tend to eat out. There's this great pizza place that has a happy hour with two-for-one beers and spicy wings. I'd like to take you there sometime. Of course, we can get you the mild wings." He winked and she smiled at his consideration.

It could be fun. She didn't leave the resort nearly enough. She opened her mouth to ask him how long he'd worked for Price Construction when his phone vibrated.

He pulled it from the clip on his belt. "I'm sorry. I have to take this, but I'll be right back."

She watched as he walked out of the dining room. From behind, he looked pretty good, until Cole stepped into her line of vision. She hated how her heart remembered him so fondly. Her body was no better, reacting to the new and improved physique, but her mind had the control. She scowled as he came to the table.

"You're hanging out with bikers now?" The disapproval in his voice got her back up. It was just like the one date she had with the man who looked down on her working at a nudist resort, like she must be desperate or something.

"Not every biker is the same, you know. I thought all cowboys were polite gentleman who stood by their woman, but then you proved me wrong."

To give him credit, he did lose the scowl and look away.

Yes, she was harsh, but he'd hurt her like no one else ever had. She hoped he felt like a loser.

His gaze returned to hers. "Point taken. So is he your latest boyfriend?" The way he said it made it sound like she was a dating fiend. The fact was, she hadn't had a serious long-term relationship with anyone since him, but he didn't need to know that.

"He could be, but we are still getting to know each other a little, so I can't honestly say yet."

His body relaxed at her statement. What did he care if she was seeing John? It was none of his business.

"You look great, Lacey." His gaze swept over her face and her body heated.

Sugar, she hated that he could do that to her. "Thanks. You've changed a lot. Sorry I didn't recognize you last night."

He shrugged. "It's been a long time, but I'd recognize you anywhere, even with the orange glow of the fire the only thing lighting your features."

Her body preened at his words, but her brain took offense. "Have you figured out how the fire started?"

He stiffened at her abrupt tone. "I just put them out. Detective Anderson will make that determination."

She tried to keep her curiosity at bay, but she couldn't resist asking. "Why did you choose to be a firefighter?"

He stared hard at her for a moment. "Because of you." He didn't explain. In fact after that cryptic response, he turned on his heel and left the dining room.

She couldn't help watching him as he left. Darn, the man looked as good from behind as from the front. She sighed. If only things had been different. If only that stupid fire in Orson had never occurred, he could still be hers.

John entered the dining room and she watched him approach. As usual his smile was wide. He pulled out his chair and sat. "Miss me?" He winked.

"Of course. No fun eating alone."

"I'm sorry. It was the office. Mr. Price got a clean-up job for this afternoon and they asked if I could do it. I said yes. If I can help Mr. Price stay afloat, I will. It's job security and I make extra money besides." He looked apologetic, but he didn't need to be.

"That's great. If I meet any local guests who are in need of Mr.

Price's services, I'd be happy to pass his name along. Does he have a brochure or something?"

John frowned. "I don't know, but I can ask. Unfortunately, for me to get this job done by nightfall, I'm going to have to leave now."

"That's okay. I have a million things to do anyway."

His smile was back as he stood. "I'll make it up to you. How about dinner sometime?"

"Sounds lovely." She smiled as he leaned over and gave her a kiss on the cheek. "I look forward to it."

"Then it's a date." He pointed to their plates. "I pay for this at the front desk, right?"

She nodded.

"Perfect. See you soon." He left the dining area with a serious jaunt in his step.

She sighed. Too bad that despite his looks and build, she felt no jitters or butterflies like she did with Cole. Was she destined to never have those feelings again?

Finishing her last bite of taco, she took another sip of tea and headed for the kitchen with her empty glass. She refilled her iced tea, narrowly avoiding Rachel. The last thing she wanted was the staff gossiping about her and Cole. No, her and John. Sugar, she needed to push Cole Hatcher out of her head.

She strolled through the main room with the huge fireplace, pondering whether to do the state taxes or the bills next. As she turned the corner to the back hall, she walked straight into a clothed man. She grabbed her glass with both hands as strong hands on her shoulders kept her from falling. She didn't need to look up to know it was Cole. His cedar scent and his bulk told her.

"Are you all right?" The concern in his voice mirrored that in his gaze as it roved over her face.

No, she wasn't all right. She was a complete mess. "Yes, I'm fine." Her breath came out as a whisper and she cleared her throat. Darn, but he had the most beautiful eyes. The bright green was streaked with tiny flecks of blue, making them hypnotizing.

"Lacey?" He lowered his head, bringing those breathtaking eyes even closer.

She could lose herself in his gaze, especially as it turned dark and his face tensed. She remembered that look. He was going to kiss her.

She tried to make her mouth form the word her heart craved, but her mind triggered a warning bell as loud as a fire alarm. As he lowered his strong chin with his firm lips toward her own, her throat finally opened.

"No." The word came out more like a caress than a command, but he stilled, his lips only inches away from hers. She swallowed. "Please don't."

He pulled back as if she'd slapped him. "Am I so odious?"

She shook her head. "I can't go there with you again, unless you can honestly tell me you believe I didn't start the fire in Orson." A glimmer of hope flamed to life in her heart as he hesitated.

Turning his hat in his hand, he met her gaze and sighed. "I can't, Lacey."

That stubborn flame of hope extinguished quickly in the pool of hurt in her chest. "Then please leave me alone."

Indecision flashed in his eyes before he nodded. Without saying another word, he donned his hat and strode out of the building.

She watched him, her teary gaze blurring the fine lines of his body and the swagger of his step. Determinedly, she straightened her shoulders and continued down the hall to relieve Kendra from the front desk.

Cole Hatcher was gone. There was no reason to worry about running into him, literally, again. She should be relieved, but the fact he still thought she'd set the fire in Orson ripped her heart's old wound wide open. At this rate, she'd be in her fifties before she was ready to trust that scarred mess to anyone again.

CHAPTER FOUR

Cole woke, his cock as hard as a newly hewed fence post. "Shit!" Another dream about Lacey. He glanced at the clock on his dresser. 1:38 a.m. He needed to stop fantasizing about her.

He threw his legs over the bed and grabbed his shorts. He didn't want to scare anyone with his nakedness since *he* didn't live on a nudist resort. It would be just his luck he'd run into his grandmother. He had plans to build a big ranch house on another part of the two thousand acre property and slowly move his operations that way so his grandparents could enjoy their retirement, but his hard-earned savings was always being raided for unexpected vet bills. Maybe if he could budget worth a damn, he could stay in the black without hitting his house fund.

He quietly crept downstairs to the kitchen, avoiding the spots on the stairs that creaked. Working strange hours at the fire station had taught him how not to wake up his grandparents.

When he entered the kitchen, he stopped and took a deep breath. The scent of peach pie still permeated the air from his grandmother's baking earlier in the day. Finally, he moved to the refrigerator and opened it. He scanned the contents, nothing really interested him since the pie was gone. Closing the door slowly, he opened the freezer.

Ah, orange popsicles. His favorite. Taking two out, he quickly stripped them of their paper and bit the tops off both. The cold, sharp taste satisfied his mouth. If he'd kept one wrapped, he could have stuck it between his legs against the damn dreams.

He should never have tried to kiss Lacey, but everything in him wanted to. At least she had stopped him. He took another bite of each popsicle, holding the cold citrus flavor in his mouth. What if Sean determined Lacey set the fire and Cole had been seen kissing her? That wouldn't look good for his career. He could see the headline of the *Wickenburg Sun*, "*Up and Coming Firefighter in Love with Arsonist.*" Yeah sure, that certainly wouldn't help his career. If he lost his job, he'd lose his horses. He couldn't let that happen.

He grabbed a napkin and took two more bites of the icy treat before navigating the stairs again. That's what he should concentrate on—selling his horses. If he could do that, he could take more in without bringing his checkbook down to the edge every month.

Dropping his shorts on the recliner in his room, he sat on the edge of the bed, sliding off the last bite from one of the popsicle sticks while holding the napkin under the other, which began to drip. He would need a new truckload of hay by month's end. Maybe he could invite Wade up to visit later in the week. He'd finish his twenty-four-hour shift at eight Wednesday morning then his four days off would start, but he didn't want to wait. He could schedule Wade for Wednesday afternoon.

Cole pulled the rest of the last orange popsicle into his mouth and threw away the sticks. He lay down, sucking hard on the ice. When would Sean know what caused the fire? What if it hadn't been Lacey? If someone else set it, could he pursue her?

His cock jerked to attention. "Fuck." There was no way she would let him near her even if that were the case. Unless he believed she had nothing to do with the fire in her parents' carriage house, she would keep him at bay, but he knew it was her. His parents had been friends of the fire chief at the time and he put the blame squarely on Lacey's shoulders. Unfortunately, now that she was so close, Cole wouldn't be able to stop thinking about her.

He had to stop. Closing his eyes, he thought about his horses, but even as he envisioned his barn and a new load of hay, his thoughts drifted to the past and making love to Lacey in his parents' barn. Her petite body flushed with desire as the hay beneath the blanket cupped her. She'd smiled up at him, her pale-pink lace bra hiding little as he gazed at her deep-rose-colored areolas and nipples dying to be freed. He skimmed his hands down her waist past her small belly button to her pink lace thong that revealed the patch of golden-blonde curls beneath it.

He loved that she enjoyed sexy underthings. He never knew what she would wear. She often teased him by telling him what she had on when they were in places where he couldn't do anything about it, like his parents' dinner table or at her parents' Christmas party.

He didn't even try to unhook the pink lace bra. Instead, he leaned over her on his elbows and with his teeth, pulled the top of the bra down until it caught under one breast. He could hear her heartbeats increase even as he let go then switched to pull the other bra cup down. Resting his chin against her ribs, he glanced at her and found her eyes turning chocolate brown with desire.

Raising his head, he stared at each nipple straining toward him. He lapped quickly across both before watching them pucker, then blew across one at time, thrilled to see the hard nubs get harder.

"Please, Cole."

He devoured her with his gaze.

She licked her lips and he couldn't resist. Gently, he brought his lips to hers and kissed her. Her arms came around his neck and he pushed his tongue into her mouth where her own met his. He slanted his head to better taste every inch of her, a slight strawberry flavor reminding him of their last hour picking the juicy fruit from his mother's garden.

Lacey's moan as she moved her hand through his hair tightened his balls with anticipation.

Releasing her mouth, he returned to her breasts. The need to taste her sweet spots was too harsh to deny. He brought his mouth to her right nipple and sucked gently. She grasped his hair as her body arched against him. The hard pearl tasted of nirvana and he nibbled it lightly before drawing it carefully into his mouth.

Lacey squeaked in pleasure, a sound all her own that had the ability to send need through him like a ricochet bullet. He couldn't wait much longer. Pulling back, he kissed his way down her flat stomach, his hands gliding along the sides of her waist and over her hips until he pushed them against her thighs, spreading her legs and revealing the wet spot of her lacy panties.

He swallowed in anticipation. Hooking his finger beneath the waistband, he pulled downward. The panty split apart, the tiny sound of Velcro as it let go caught his attention. Surprised, he looked up at her, but her face had changed.

She wasn't the innocent, young, loving Lacey he'd known. This was the more mature Lacey with refined features. This was the face of a woman who knew what she wanted and the smirk on her lips told him loud and clear, she wanted him. He let his gaze roam over her full breasts, held now by a bright, hot pink underwire bra with no cups at all, serving up her woman's chest like a feast that couldn't be ignored.

Unable to resist, he latched on to a nipple and sucked hard. Lacey's hands fisted in his hair as she arched toward his mouth. He couldn't let go, sucking and twirling his tongue across the hard nub. He used one hand to knead the other breast before twirling that nipple with his fingers, even as he nibbled the one inside his mouth.

"Cole." His name coming from her lips was like a caress. It was time.

He released her breast to go back to the sweet spot he had unveiled. The hot-pink panty remained partially opened, and he pulled back one side to view what he hadn't seen in years. Her sweet pink softness was moist with her readiness, but her folds were closed tight, revealing nothing.

He pushed his hands against her inner thighs, spreading her wider, parting her folds a tiny bit. He held her legs apart and brought his mouth to the slit that opened and from the bottom to the top, he tasted her need until he hit the hard ridge of her clit. Slowly, he licked, circling it and lapping upward.

Lacey's hips rose from the hay, rocking against his mouth.

Leisurely, as if his cock weren't as hard as ironwood and his balls tighter than a rattlesnake's grip, he brought his tongue down between her folds and pushed his way into the opening of her sheath.

"Cole, I need you inside me, now." Lacey's hands gripped his hair, trying to pull him up. Willingly he gave into her, his cock jerking at the remembered tightness that was all her.

Covering her now full curvy body with his own, he hesitated. He was so much bigger now.

Her hands on his ass, fingers digging into his flesh, convinced him to give it a try for both their sakes.

He pushed the head of his cock between her slick folds and pressed himself an inch into the tight canal he remembered. "Shit, Lacey, you still feel so good."

Her legs wrapped around his. "Don't stop. Please, Cole."

She pulled him in another inch, her sheath sucking him hard, causing him to take deep breaths to keep control. He let his head fall forward, lightly touching her forehead with his own. "I don't want to hurt you."

Her body stiffened and her eyes opened. "You've already done that."

A bucket of ice water spilled over his head and he sputtered, his whole body tensing as he sat up in bed. No water. No Lacey. Just another fucking dream. He looked at the clock and moaned. 2:47 a.m. Two more hours before he had to get up. He punched the pillow and lay back down, his hands behind his head. What the hell would it take to get just an hour of uninterrupted sleep?

~~~~~

Lacey coughed and kicked off the blanket. Sitting up, she

grabbed the bottle of water on her nightstand and took a gulp. She pulled in deep breaths, counting to ten on the inhale, counting to ten on the exhale like she'd been taught. No smoke filled her lungs as it had in her dream. No fire licked up the wall next to the door to get out. No heat blasted her face, just the cooling flow of the air conditioner. She lifted the hem of her t-shirt and wiped her neck.

She was safe.

Cole had brought back her nightmares.

She took another swallow of water. It had taken her two months to stop them the first time. Reliving the nightmare of waking up in the burning carriage house every night was not conducive to coherent thought. She'd lose her job if she didn't get a handle on them.

She shouldn't be having nightmares at all. According to the therapist her parents insisted she see, the fact she had wrapped herself in a blanket and got herself out through the flaming door should have convinced her mind she was in control. But she'd never told the therapist about Cole, or that the need to see him again had motivated her to brave the fire to get out. Nor had she told the woman that he held her closely afterward only to push her out of his life the next day.

Lacey swung her legs over the side of the bed and slipped her feet into the pink bunny slippers her mom had insisted on buying her. She pulled on her peach silk robe and padded into the kitchen. Turning on the light over the stove, she set the tea kettle to boil and prepared to make chamomile tea. Maybe the tea and looking over the monthly budget could calm her mind enough to sleep a couple more hours. It was only 3:05 a.m. and if she showed up to work any earlier than five thirty, she'd hear about it.

Luckily, her casita faced the main building, so she didn't have a view of the burnt rubble. When her tea was ready, she walked outside onto her patio, her computer under her arm, but it was chillier than she'd expected. Maybe a warmer robe was in order. Fall was such a great time of year because the temperatures finally dropped at night.

As she set her computer and tea on the table, movement caught her eye. Someone crept around the back of the resort's kitchen and he or she was clearly looking for a way in. No guest would attempt to obtain something to eat by climbing in a window.

Quietly, she moved back inside and picked up her phone, dialing Kendra, who she sincerely hoped wasn't still in her office.

"Lacey, are you all right?" Kendra was definitely wide awake.

"Yes, I'm fine. Are you in your office?"

"No, I'm home. Why?"

"I just saw someone trying to get into the kitchen from the back of the main building."

"Shit!" Kendra must have covered the phone because Lacey heard a muffled conversation. "Okay, Wade and I will check it out. You stay put and lock your doors and windows."

Lock her doors and windows? Fear meandered up her spine. Maybe she should bring her laptop in first. That had too much confidential information to leave out on her patio with a prowler about. Hands sweating, she quietly opened the patio door and grabbed her computer. Jumping back into her home, she closed the door quickly and locked it.

Not sure if she'd locked the windows last time she used them, she checked each one, glad she did when she found the one over the kitchen sink unlocked. She'd locked the front door when she came home, but she double-checked anyway.

Leaving the light on in her living room, she moved into her dark bedroom and closed the door then stood next to her window where she could see both Kendra's two-story home and the main building.

Wade strode down the path to the new building then broke into a run. He must have seen something. She watched him until he passed out of view. Now she wished Kendra *had* hired a security guard. It was easy to believe they were so far off the beaten path that no one would bother them, but most people in the area knew they existed and with police at least twenty minutes away, that left a long time for someone to escape if they wanted to steal something or do damage. Kendra had already had graffiti issues on the guest garage, and an attempt to destroy the bridge across the creek.

Lacey kept her eyes peeled for Wade, getting more nervous as each minute ticked by. Then the lights flicked on inside and outside the main building. Gosh, she hoped that was Wade.

The phone ringing in her living room startled her and she put her hand to her chest, even as she ran out to get it.

"Hello?"

"Lacey? Wade. Whoever was snooping about is gone but the side window to the generator room was busted. Not sure they had enough time to take anything, but could you come over and take a look? Make sure everything is the way you left it?"

"Of course. Let me get some clothes on." She heard glass smashing in the background. "Are you all right?"

"I'm fine. Just walking on glass over here. You wait until Kendra comes by and picks you up. I don't want anyone alone out here while it's still dark."

"Okay." When Wade hung up, she returned to her bedroom

and threw on a pale-yellow sundress. Where was her white shrug? She liked to have it with her at work because of the air-conditioning. Not finding it in her closet, she gave up and grabbed her lavender wrap instead. She probably left her shrug in the office. After brushing her teeth, she braided her hair and grabbed her straw cowboy hat. At least she didn't have to worry about sleeping anymore.

The low hum of a golf cart caught her attention as she slipped on a pair of sandals. She donned her cowboy hat and made it to the door before Kendra could knock. In the light of her front door, she could see Adriana, the bartender, was already on the cart. Adriana gave a smirk. "Hope you weren't looking forward to a full night's sleep."

Lacey shook her head as she jumped in the back seat of the cart. "I was planning to come into work early today anyway."

Kendra started the cart moving toward the biggest building on the resort.

Adriana growled. "Not me. As soon as I check to see if anything is missing, I'm going back to bed. I don't have to work until noon, and there's a good chance I might be late."

Kendra frowned, but didn't say anything. It was probable neither Adriana nor Kendra had gone to bed yet. Both usually didn't start work until noon, but Kendra as the owner did whatever needed to be done, when it needed to be done.

Wade greeted them at the front doors then locked them after they entered. "Lacey, check the front desk, safe and computers. Adriana, check the bar and see if anything is missing." He took Kendra's hand. "I'll show you the break-in."

Adriana headed for the two bar areas and Lacey watched

Kendra and Wade stride through the gathering room with the large stone fireplace. She sighed. A tiny bit of her was jealous of their relationship, but mostly she was glad they had moved past their different backgrounds and planned to make a life together.

She checked out the front desk to see if anything was disturbed from the outside first. Seeing nothing, she walked down the hall and entered the back room with the coffeemaker. Flipping the switch, she scanned the area but didn't see anything amiss.

She checked the petty cash and computers at the front desk. Nothing was disturbed there either. Maybe the prowler didn't have time to take anything. Comfortable that all was as she left it, she traveled farther down the hallway to Kendra's office and crouched by the safe. Quickly moving the dial in the correct combination, she opened it and counted the money, twice. It was all there.

She closed the safe and spun the dial before standing. As she headed down the hallway back toward the front, she heard Adriana shout and curse.

Lacey broke into a run and met Kendra and Wade as they, too, ran to the bar. Adriana stood behind the bar scowling. Kendra hopped up onto the ironwood bar top. "What is it?"

"Those motherfuckers took at least a dozen top shelf bottles of booze. Excuse my language, Lacey."

"No problem. I think it was warranted in this case."

Kendra hopped over to the inside of the bar and reviewed the missing bottles. "I know liquor is expensive, but who would do this?"

Lacey sat on one of the barstools and peered over. "Probably poor college students stocking up for the coming weekend."

Kendra's eyes turned hard. "They have high-end taste for poor college students."

"Of course." She thought back to the college parties she'd attended. "Sapphire Blue Gin, Patron Silver Tequila and Jägermeister were the norm, but it's been a few years so tastes may have changed. Besides, if you couldn't afford liquor and had the chance to steal some, wouldn't you steal the stuff you could never afford and buy the stuff you could?"

"She has a point." Wade leaned against the bar, his stance reminding her of Cole's.

Did they all go to cowboy school and learn that? She clasped her hands in front of her.

"Shit." Adriana pushed her disheveled black hair away from her face. "All those you rattled off are missing and then some. I have back-up bottles in the storage room if they didn't hit that, but we'll have to order more."

They all looked at each other then as one turned and headed for the storage room. When they arrived, Kendra opened the door and hit the light switch. They all stepped in. Lacey scanned the shelves and breathed a sigh of relief. "You can double-check with Selma, but I think everything is here."

Adrianna stalked to the boxes of booze. "Yeah, none of these have been disturbed."

Kendra threw her hands up. "I guess that's that. I'll call Detective Anderson and ask him to come out. Who knows? This could be related to the fire." She looked at Lacey before brushing by. "Adriana, make a list of everything that was taken. But don't touch anything until after Detective Anderson has had a look."

They filed out, Adriana cursing as she closed the door.

Lacey followed. "Look at it this way, Adriana. After you make a list, you can go back to bed."

The hot Hispanic bartender looked over her shoulder at her. "You mean go to bed in the first place." She winked and sauntered off toward the bar.

Lacey chuckled. Adriana may not be working in a brothel anymore, but she enjoyed one-night stands even more now that sex was no longer business and all pleasure. She and Adriana were complete opposites, yet they truly enjoyed each other's company. It was what made Poker Flat so unique. Kendra may have pulled together a family of misfits, but what a great family to be a part of.

She returned to the staff room behind the front desk and started a pot of coffee. She scanned the area again to be sure nothing was missing. She doubted very much the theft of the liquor and the fire the night before were related. Then again, they had dealt with vandals before. Still, it felt good that Kendra expected the fire's cause to be anything but her.

Lacey's heart hitched again at Cole's betrayal. It had been years since she'd felt the hiccups of pain over his quick judgement. Why did he have to come back into her life? And more importantly, would he stay out of it?

"I smell coffee." Kendra walked in and pulled a coffee mug out of the cabinet. "Looks like I'm destined to go without sleep for another day." She sat at the small round table waiting for the coffee to finish brewing.

"I'm sorry." Lacey sat across from her. "I thought our troubles were over once the resort opened."

Kendra shook her head. "I didn't. People just can't stand alternative lifestyles. They are so insecure in what they believe, they must make everyone conform in order to feel safe."

Lacey pondered Kendra's opinion. "I never thought of it that way. So basically, some people in this county feel having a hidden resort for nudists means that their own lifestyle may be threatened? How strange."

Kendra shrugged. "I don't expect to change anyone's mind. It's like politics and religion. A subject that will always have conflict. All I want is for others to leave my guests alone. I want a safe environment for them. This latest incident reinforces the need for me to hire a security guard, maybe two."

"As long as neither is like Powell." Lacey smirked. "I think we need someone with a little more backbone."

"Believe me. This time the interviews will be more like interrogations." The coffeemaker beeped and Kendra stood. "Why don't you call Dale and ask him to closely vet a few candidates for me." She poured coffee into her mug. "Unless I have you start the process, it'll never happen."

"Will do. I'll call him today. I know *I* will feel safer."

Her boss nodded and headed for the door but stopped and turned. "I'd be lost without you, Lacey. Thank you for keeping this place so organized."

"You're welcome." Warmth suffused her cheeks as Kendra disappeared. She rose and pulled a mug out of the cabinet for herself. Praise from her boss didn't come often and it always took her by surprise. She was paid very well, had her own little casita to live in and loved her work. She couldn't ask for anything else.

"I almost forgot." Kendra stuck her head in. "Detective Anderson said he planned to come out today anyway to interview the staff about the fire. If you could spread the word, that would be helpful."

She swallowed hard. "I will." When Kendra disappeared, Lacey collapsed into the chair. Living through another fire investigation opened too many old wounds and frazzled her nerves.

Taking a deep breath, she rose, poured herself a cup of coffee and took a much needed sip. Time to make a to-do list for today. She couldn't call anyone yet as it was far too early. She glanced at the clock. 3:37 a.m. It would be a long day.

~~~~~~

Lacey watched as Detective Anderson flipped the page of paper over the top of his pad. "I did find tracks past the barrier on the other side. It looks like whoever was here came down on an ATV. I took fingerprints from the bar. We should know whether there were one or two people even if the prints aren't perfect."

"I only saw one." Lacey looked at Kendra. "Wish I had woken sooner."

Detective Anderson's steady gaze turned to her. "And why did you wake up then? Did you hear something?"

She shook her head. "No. I just had a bad dream and decided to have a cup of tea on my patio before going back to sleep."

He looked at her oddly before scribbling on his pad.

If he had had the same kind of dream she had, he wouldn't have wanted to go back to sleep right away either.

"Do you think there's a connection between the fire and this theft?" Kendra brought the detective's gaze back to her.

"It's too early to tell yet. I found an empty bottle of Tequila at the burn site, as well as a piece of clothing which looks to be a female's."

Kendra smirked. "Can't say many of our female guests wear clothing, but some do bring something to cover their shoulders because of the air-conditioning, though I can't imagine them hanging out at the construction site unless…"

"Unless what?" The detective's gaze turned sharp.

"Unless the guest was flirting with one of the construction workers." She looked over at Lacey and wiggled her brows.

Lacey felt heat rise to her cheeks. The detective studied her, so she explained. "What she's intimating is that sometimes I delivered Selma's snacks to the construction crew, and there's a gentleman there who I conversed with."

"And had lunch with yesterday." Kendra nodded approvingly.

She looked at her boss. "I don't think the detective really cares about my love life."

"I might."

She snapped her gaze back to him and quickly checked his left hand. A well-worn gold band was evident on his ring finger. She met his steady gaze with her own. "Why?"

He ignored her question and spoke to Kendra. "I will need to talk to each staff member separately."

"That's not a problem." Kendra laid her hand on Lacey's shoulder. "Lacey can let you know where everyone is, depending on the time."

"Good. And I will also need the contact information for the guests who were here the night of the fire."

Kendra stiffened. "You think a guest could have set it?"

"I don't know yet, but I need to cover all bases."

"If you don't have to contact my guests, I'd prefer you didn't." Kendra raised her hand as the detective opened his mouth. "I understand you may need to. All I'm saying is if the trail leads elsewhere, I prefer they not be bothered. Is there any chance the fire wasn't started by human means?"

Detective Anderson shook his head. "No. It was definitely started by someone. This was no lightning strike or electrical arc."

Kendra's shoulders fell and Lacey laid her hand on her boss's arm. "Don't worry. None of your current staff would ever do anything to harm Poker Flat."

"So there has been trouble with staff before?" Detective Anderson's shrewd blue gaze zeroed in on her.

Darn. Her stupid loose tongue. "There was one person. He was let go. He may have bad feelings, but I believe he's in jail at the moment." She pinned Anderson with her own gaze until he backed down. So there. It would be tough to start a fire from jail.

The detective scribbled more in his pad before flipping to a new blank page. "I might as well start with you." He looked directly at her before turning to Kendra. "I'll talk to you next and then the bartender."

Kendra took the hint that Anderson wanted her to leave and she stood. "I'll check in with Adriana. She may still be asleep. It's been a long two days for all of us." She stared hard at the officer, but Lacey doubted he cared what she thought or how much sleep they'd had. He probably figured if they were tired they would slip up and give themselves away.

Her gut twisted as familiar pains roiled through her stomach. She'd hated being accused of something she hadn't done back in Orson, but now this detective appeared to be accusing everyone on staff. She hoped in the end the fire was caused by anyone but a staff person, just to prove that working at a nudist resort didn't mean they had no morals.

"Do you own a white shrug?"

She snapped her attention back to Anderson. "Yes, I do. I couldn't find it this morning. Why?"

He didn't even write that down on his pad. "Because I found it at the burn site."

No. No. Not again!

CHAPTER FIVE

Cole tamped down the need to shout like a teenager who just got the girl of his dreams to go to the prom with him. It looked like he'd be selling four good horses to the Poker Flat resort. He led Elsa out of her stall toward Wade, who was inspecting Romeo. "He's a mellow horse and should work perfectly for new riders."

"What was wrong with him? He looks as good as Sam." Wade moved to the other side of Romeo.

"He suffered from malnutrition. Poor guy was only days from collapsing. The re-feeding was touch and go for a while especially in the first month. If my grandfather wasn't here, this horse would have never made it because I work twenty-four-hour shifts at the fire station and Romeo needed a constant watch."

Wade pet the quarter horse's nose and the animal leaned his head toward him. "How long have you had him?"

Cole tied Elsa and stepped closer to give Romeo a pat. "He's been with us ten months now. He's been eating well for four months and his weight has remained constant. He's ready to move on. If he stays here much longer, he'll get fat from lack of activity."

Wade looked up at that then shook his head. "I doubt that. You have a nice spread here. I'm sure Romeo could get plenty of exercise."

"Possibly, but he likes to be ridden and I'm too busy to spend the time needed to be sure all these horses get the right amount of exercise. And my grandparents are getting up there in years. Though they both still ride, I can't expect them to exercise *all* the horses."

Wade stepped around Romeo. "I see your dilemma. But there will always be more abused and abandoned horses. How will you keep them healthy?"

Cole didn't meet Wade's gaze, instead focusing on Romeo. "I have a long-term plan, which includes staff. I'm still working out the kinks in between caring for the horses I have and my job." What he really needed was a financial manager who could help him keep everything straight.

"I'll definitely take him." Wade walked over to Elsa. "Who do we have here?"

"That's Elsa. She's the only Arabian I have at the moment."

Wade let the horse greet him and gently patted her side. "She has a lot of scars."

Cole swallowed. Cases like Elsa's were the toughest. "She'd been badly burned in a wildfire. The owners were going to put her down, but I offered to take her off their hands. They were happy to let me have her."

Wade whistled low. "I'm surprised she made it. What made you take her?"

"It was her eyes. She was standing there with so much burned skin, shaking in fear, but she didn't run. All she did was stand and look at me as if asking me to help her. I couldn't ignore that." He didn't know how else to explain the feeling he had when he'd seen her.

"I understand." Wade nodded.

In that moment Cole was absolutely sure that selling her to Wade would ensure her a caring home. That was important to him because she had a special place in his heart.

"Is she why you became a firefighter?" Wade's question surprised him.

"No, I've only had her three years. No one wants a horse that looks so ragged even though she's as healthy as can be and incredibly docile."

"But it was a horse, wasn't it, that caused you to become a firefighter?"

Cole leaned against the barn wall and crossed his arms. "Yeah, a horse was a big part of it. His name was King. He didn't make it." Cole swallowed, the pain of losing that horse after trying so hard to save it still knotted up his stomach. Wade didn't interrupt, his empathy clear in his silence.

Eventually, Cole's stomach loosened and he continued, leaving out Lacey and her fire's influence on his decision. "When I told my parents I didn't want to breed horses but save them, they hit the roof."

"I bet they did." Wade's chuckle relaxed Cole a bit more.

He shrugged. "I wasn't surprised." Though he had been hurt at their refusal to help him at all. Instead they promised his younger brother their ranch. "But my grandparents had this cattle ranch and had sold off the last of their cattle to enjoy their retirement. They were even thinking of selling this place. When I told them what I wanted to do, they fell in love with the idea. Actually, I think they were getting a little bored and my venture gave them new purpose."

Wade left Elsa and stood in front of him. "I think it's time to talk price, and a beer if you have one."

Cole dropped his arms. "You want Romeo and Elsa?"

"I want them and the two quarter horses you showed me first, Blaze and Bella. Once I get them settled in, I'm pretty sure I'll be back for more."

Cole grinned, unable to contain his joy. That his horses would be appreciated was always a thrill, but in Wade he saw someone who believed strongly in what he was doing here. He hadn't seen that since the day his grandparents had offered him their ranch. "Then I think I can find a beer or two."

As he led the way to the front porch, his mind raced with possible prices and what the cash flow could do for Last Chance Ranch. "Make yourself comfortable. I'll get the beer."

After taking two bottles from the fridge, he grabbed a bag of tortilla chips and a jar of homemade salsa and strode back to the porch. "I brought a snack in case you had the munchies. It's not half as good as Selma's food, but I finished my grandmother's pumpkin bread yesterday."

"That's fine. I'm not sure anything can live up to Selma's cooking. She's spoiled us. Kendra and I never go out to eat because we always compare the food to Selma's." Wade twisted the top from his beer and took a swallow.

Cole did the same. "Do you think you'll be able to use Elsa for trail riding?"

"Of course. That's what all these horses will be used for. They have the right temperament. Why? Is there something I should know about her?"

"No, it's just that, she's not the prettiest horse. I wasn't sure if your guests would balk at riding her."

Wade shook his head as a grin spread across his face. "You have it backward. I'll bet she'll be the most requested horse."

Cole frowned. "I don't understand."

"I don't imagine you do. I wouldn't have either, but running a nudist resort opens your eyes to a lot of things." Wade took another swallow and stared at the desert land. "Our guests, the nudists, are very accepting of the non-perfect. In fact they appear to embrace it. Even Kendra didn't realize that before she opened, but the fact is, having a staff of less-than-perfect people has endeared them to the guests."

Cole remained silent. He didn't view Lacey as "non-perfect," especially in looks. Then again his ex-girlfriend did have a reputation for starting fires. To be fair, one fire. The jury was still out on the latest, but what were the chances?

Wade returned his gaze to Cole. "Elsa will be in high demand because she isn't perfect. She will be accepted as much as Sundancer or Romeo. That's what's so great about the nudist community. Looks don't matter."

"Then I'm glad she's found a real home." Cole raised his bottle. "To Poker Flat Nudist Resort."

They clinked bottles and took a swallow.

"If you don't mind, I'd like to pick the horses up in a week or so, but don't worry, I'll pay you as soon as we agree on a price."

Cole raised a brow. "Why do you want to wait so long? I

thought you said you had a lot of guests coming in next week and needed the additional horses."

"I did and do, but we had a break-in Monday night and I want to wait now until the security guards have been hired."

"Break-in?" Was Lacey okay? "Is everyone all right?"

"Yeah. They broke into the main building when no one was there and stole some high-end booze." Wade held up his bottle, which was anything but top shelf. "If Lacey hadn't seen the intruder, they might have gotten away with a lot more."

"Lacey?"

"Yeah. She woke around three and noticed someone skulking around the back of the building. The thieves heard me coming and ran out the front door. I chased them, but they had an ATV and took off. So I'd like to wait a week or two unless Detective Anderson makes an arrest beforehand."

Cole felt sweat form on his brow. Just the thought of Lacey in trouble had him on edge. For eight years, he didn't know where she was or what she did, but now that he'd seen her again, he couldn't ignore the plain fact that he still loved her, no matter what she'd done. And this time, he didn't have his parents reminding him every day how dangerous she was to both him and his family's reputation.

~~~~~

"Hey, Sean, mind if I come in?" Cole leaned against the doorway of Detective Anderson's office, trying to look casual when every muscle in his body was tense.

Sean looked up from his computer. "Sure. What can I do for you, Cole?"

He sat in the chair at the side of Sean's desk. "I was just heading over to the nudist resort. They're buying a few horses from me and I thought I'd stop by and see if you'd come up with anything regarding the fire." He didn't want Sean to know he'd already heard about the burglary.

"I can tell you this." Sean leaned back in his chair and rested his ankle on his knee. "It was started by someone. I just don't know who or if burning down the new building was intentional."

"Any leads at all?"

"Too many. I have vandals who may be the same as those who broke in there the next night or completely different ones. I have a bottle of top shelf tequila that belonged to somebody, and I have Lacey Winters' sweater, half burned at the site. The only thing I don't have is a single suspect."

Cole felt like someone slapped him upside the head at the mention of Lacey. He should have known, but a side of him wanted to believe her innocent. How was she dealing with it this time? Would she run away like she had before? He stood, the need to see her again too strong to ignore. "Well, if there's anything I can do to help, let me know."

He expected Sean to say he had this, but instead he just stared at him and then a gleam came into his eye. Oh shit. Why did Cole feel like he wasn't going to like Sean's response?

"You said you're heading out there right now?"

"Yeah."

Sean leaned back in his chair. "Do me a favor. See if you can have a casual discussion with some of the employees. I'd like to get your read on them. Nothing official, but another set of eyes couldn't hurt."

He should come clean and tell Sean he didn't want Lacey found guilty, even if she was, but he couldn't do it. Instead, he mumbled a quick "sure" and left before Sean could ask him anything else.

What the hell was he doing? He'd never withheld information before. Had he changed that much over the years or were his feelings for Lacey coloring his judgement? Shit, he had no idea.

Stalking out of the police station, he refused to acknowledge the protective instincts permeating his brain. He had to go to Poker Flat and see her, maybe even see if she still had any feelings for him.

He grimaced as he jumped in his Silverado 3500 pickup truck. There was a good chance the only feeling she had for him was hate, but even that was better than indifference. It'd been three days since she'd seen him. Maybe she'd mellowed a bit. It had been quite a shock for both of them.

His gut told him they needed another chance. He turned the truck onto the highway and sped toward Poker Flat. Maybe it was their last chance, but she'd been his perfect match back in high school. Maybe like Wade said, he needed to open his mind to her imperfection.

~~~~~

Lacey closed Kendra's office door after showing the second candidate in for an interview. Wade's friend Dale, who owned the temp agency Kendra used, had lined up six candidates for the two security guard positions.

Too bad hiring them wouldn't help her sleep through the night. She was plagued with dreams of the fire, only they'd changed. Instead of waking up when she burst through the door, they continued with Cole calling her name as he fought the fire until the building collapsed on him. She should have never watched the construction site until the building collapsed. Now her mind combined the two fires, sending fear racing through her body every night.

She walked back to the front desk to find another candidate waiting for her. The black-haired man with bulging biceps stretching his black t-shirt gave himself away by the fact he was clothed, but he hadn't exactly dressed for an interview. He hadn't even taken off his black cowboy hat, which was strange. It was as if he didn't really want the job.

"Hi, can I help you?"

He didn't quite look at her. "Yeah. Hunter McKade. Dale Osborn sent me."

She glanced down at her list and checked him off. At least he was on time, early in fact. "If you'd like to take a seat over there, I will call you when Ms. Lowe is ready for you."

He nodded once then turned and walked toward the dining room, completely ignoring her instructions. As he walked away she could see he also wore black jeans and black cowboy boots that made no sound on the hard floor.

The man was definitely odd. She shook her head. If he forgot to come back, it would just make Kendra's selection that much easier.

The lobby door opened again and Billy came in. "Afternoon, Lacey."

She smiled. "Good afternoon, Billy." The older man had a special place in her heart. He was so sweet. "Selma has your lunch all boxed up."

"Yeehaw." The man gave her a toothy grin as he strode a bit lopsidedly toward the dining room

Uh-oh. He'd been drinking during work hours again. She'd have to talk to him before Kendra found out. Not that her boss wasn't aware of Billy's problem, but they had a deal. As long as he could function in his position, Kendra would keep him on. He did well for a week or so and then would forget he couldn't drink during work. Lacey made it her responsibility to sit him down and remind him. She couldn't see anyone else hiring him.

In no time, Billy had his lunch and was meandering back to his golf cart. She watched him disappear down the hill and reappear on the other side of the ravine. At least he wasn't weaving.

Turning away from the counter, she sat at her computer and ordered the food Selma needed for next week. The woman was a marvelous cook, but she didn't even know where the "on" switch was when it came to computers.

She finished all Selma's requested items then added a few more Adriana would need. The bartender didn't write anything down, just walked by once in a while and hollered out what she'd need next time Lacey ordered "stuff."

She hovered the mouse over the "send" button then moved it away and added another item. Popsicles. For some reason she craved popsicles. She hadn't had them in months. Finishing her order, she sent it off through cyberspace.

The sun's reflection off a tan golf cart caught her attention through the lobby's floor-to-ceiling windows. Billy pulled to a stop before the front doors and dropped off another clothed person, probably another security guard candidate. She looked around the lobby. The other applicant wasn't back yet.

As the new arrival opened the door to the lobby, her heart picked up speed, even as her muscles stiffened.

Cole took his hat off, his cowboy stride causing her gaze to drop to his blue jeans. Her cheeks flushed as her mind conjured up what his legs must look like underneath the denim material now that he'd grown up.

She returned her gaze to her computer, determined to ignore him. Why was he here again?

"Lacey."

Her name coming from his lips had always made her want to melt, especially when he said it with such yearning, like he did now. Unable to be rude, she turned her head to look at him. She *could* keep this completely professional. "Yes, Cole."

The right side of his lips quirked up a tiny bit, as if he knew she was trying to ignore him and losing her battle.

"Can you come out here so we can talk?"

"What do we have to talk about? I'm a little busy."

His lips lost their slight curve. "It won't take long."

"Very well." She heaved an exaggerated sigh and took her time getting up to walk toward the back room. Once beyond his sight, she smoothed down her pale-pink skirt that fell to the tops of her white cowboy boots. Quickly, she looked in the small mirror inside the broom closet to make sure her braid was still presentable, its golden color blending with the yellow and pink flowers on her blouse. She needed to remember he'd given up on her without even hearing her side of the story.

She closed the closet door and put one hand over her heart. "Now behave." Straightening her shoulders, she stepped out to meet Cole.

When she came around the corner to face him, it was as if she were being pulled forward by a stampede of wild horses. It took all her willpower to stop a couple feet in front of him and not walk directly into his arms. *Remember, he still thinks you set the fire. He dumped you.*

He examined her from head to toe as if looking for something. "Are you okay?"

"Of course. Why wouldn't I be?" His look of concern was genuine. She'd give him that.

"I heard there was a theft and that you saw the perpetrators. They haven't come back, have they? They don't know you saw them, do they?"

It hadn't occurred to her that the thieves would come back or might look for her. "I'm fine. No one saw me." She tried to ignore his woodsy scent as the ceiling fans wafted it over her. It brought back so many memories.

He touched her cheek, startling her from her thoughts.

"But how are you holding up? I heard you are a suspect…"

Again. He didn't say it, but she heard it in his voice. "So what? I'm used to that. Just remember, being a suspect and doing the deed are two very different things, Cole Hatcher."

He pulled his hand away from her face at her tone and frowned. "Why was your sweater at the construction site?"

She tensed. "Why don't you ask Detective Anderson? I already told him."

"Because I want to hear it from you."

Why? To judge if she was lying? Fine. "If you must know, I wore it that day against the chill of the air-conditioning in here as I had a sleeveless dress on. When I went out to visit John… You remember John Lockhart from lunch the other day? After talking to him for a while I grew hot, so I threw it on a pile of lumber stacked outside the building. When I returned to the front desk I forgot about it. That was the Friday before the fire." She clasped her hands in front of her. "I had no reason to go back to the construction site since John wasn't working the weekend. I didn't realize it was missing until the day after the fire." She shrugged nonchalantly, loving the way his mouth drew into a straight line at the mention of John. If Cole thought there was more between her and the construction worker, that was his fault.

He remained quiet like he expected her to start blabbing something else, but there was nothing else to tell.

"I believe you."

Her eyes widened as her chest constricted, making her words come out in a whisper. "You do?"

Cole smiled sadly. "Is that really so hard to believe?"

That wasn't exactly the answer she expected, but her heart completely overruled her head and she wrapped her arms around his neck and pulled him down for a kiss.

Every nerve ending in her body woke as if from a long sleep as Cole's lips slanted over her own and his tongue met hers. Her world became whole again when his large arms pulled her against his hard chest. He was so familiar, his cedar scent, his deep kiss, the excitement that had her nipples paying attention, but he was new, different, and so big.

He pulled his tantalizing mouth away and gazed into her eyes. "Lacey, I want to help."

Huh? He could help by bringing his strong lips back to hers.

"We need to discover who started the fire."

In a split second her brain had control again and she tried to pull out of his arms, but he wasn't letting go.

"Wait, Lacey. What's wrong?"

"Let me go." She couldn't believe he was thinking about the fire while kissing her. Had he developed a one-track mind? She liked him better when he was younger and the track he was on was more to her liking.

"I believe the lady told you to let her go." The deep voice behind her stopped her struggles and she looked over her shoulder.

"Oh, Mr. McKade." She glanced back at Cole. He looked ready to tear the man apart. An exquisite and purely feminine thrill sped down her spine.

She turned back to Mr. McKade. He didn't show any emotion at all, even more stoic than Kendra before Wade came into her life. This man was too calm and yet very alert. "It's okay. Cole and I go way back." She wrapped her arms as far around Cole as she could.

The man moved his gaze from her to Cole, who looked like he would happily pound Mr. McKade into the floor.

"Cole." She had to use her hand to tap his cheek in order to catch his attention. "Cole. Mr. McKade's presence reminds me that another candidate is due to come out of Kendra's office at any moment and it's not exactly appropriate for us to be, um, engaged with each other in the lobby."

Her pretty little speech made no impression on him at all and as soon as she finished talking, he raised his gaze. "Where'd he go?" In that instant, he let her go and turned to look around the lobby.

Mr. McKade was gone. She shook her head. As if a disappearing job candidate weren't bad enough, she couldn't recapture Cole's attention. She threw her hands up and walked to the back room, so she could man the front desk again.

"Lacey." Cole's cowboy boots clicked along the tile floor behind her, his stride long and confident.

There was way too much to like about Cole Hatcher, especially now that he believed her. She yearned to give into him, but could she trust him with her heart again? She shivered. That wasn't something she wanted to contemplate.

Cole stepped into the back room.

She held up her hand. "You can't come back here."

He strode toward her. "Why not? We need to talk and you can see the front desk from here. Besides, I'm not leaving until I set Mr. Cash straight."

"Mr. Cash?"

Cole motioned toward the lobby with his head. "The disappearing man in all black out there."

"Oh, Mr. McKade. I probably should look for him. It's almost time for his interview." She stepped toward the door, but Cole wouldn't let her pass.

"No. He can find his own way to the interview, if that's really why he's here. You and I need to figure out who set the fire at the new construction site."

She stepped back. "Why?"

"Because I don't want you accused again. Please, work with me on this. I know about your sweater—"

"Shrug."

"Okay, shrug. That's the strangest name for a piece of clothing. I understand an empty bottle of tequila was found at the site as well. Did any of the construction workers drink on the sly?"

She frowned, taking a seat at the small table. "If you're asking if John drinks, the answer is yes, but he prefers beer and no, he didn't drink on the job."

"I didn't mean just him." Cole squinted at nothing in particular. "What about the other workers? When you brought Selma's snacks, did you notice anyone drinking?"

"Oh." Had anyone left the group when she brought the food? "No, no one slipped away while I was there, but I didn't stay long. Maybe twenty minutes."

"That's all the time you needed to flirt with John?"

She flushed, thrilled by his irritated voice. There was definitely jealousy behind it. "If it wasn't one of the construction workers, it may have been the same people who stole booze the other night. I told Kendra I think it's college-age people."

Cole flipped the chair next to her around and straddled it to face her, his large forearm crossed over the top. "Can you think of anyone who would have an issue with the new building being built? What was it anyway?"

"It was one side of an Old West town." She smiled, excited to explain the project she'd suggested to Kendra. "The idea is to have it look like a real western town from the 1800s but instead of a brothel, we have a massage station. Instead of a bank, we have a workout room. Instead of a saloon, we have Native American gifts."

"So this would bring more staff to Poker Flat."

She shook her head. "No. These would be rented out spaces. Kendra doesn't want to have to oversee that as well."

Cole sat back. "So if someone didn't like the fact that Kendra was planning to rake in more money, they might burn it down."

"I guess. But I'm not sure how many people know her. She's stayed away from town officials since Wade became manager. She only deals with the contractors. She's a hard negotiator. I even heard Mr. Price complaining about how tough she was." Lacey grinned, her pride in her boss growing every day.

"Price didn't like his contract?"

"I think he just liked to complain about it, though he said he would negotiate differently when it was time to rebuild. I'm glad we insured the new construction. At least we won't lose money on rebuilding."

"But Price will make more money. He's a small construction company. Have you heard how stable he is?"

Lacey clasped her hands. It felt like she'd be betraying a confidence if she told Cole what John had said. "I know he has a clean-up business on the side. He complained more about the timeline than anything else. He seemed pretty stunned when I told him there'd been a fire."

"I wish I could have seen that."

"But even if he was tight on money, that doesn't mean he caused the fire. Lots of small businesses struggle and never do something like that." Mr. Price's reaction to the news of the fire was too honest for her to think he had something to do with it.

Cole rose. "That's true, but it could go toward motivation. I need to talk to Wade about the horses he ordered, but I was wondering if you were free tonight. I'd like to catch up on all that has happened to you since I last saw you."

Part of her wanted to squeal, but the other part was afraid to trust herself being with him. "I don't know. Maybe after this fire investigation is over."

He opened his mouth to speak but closed it. Instead, he walked to the door before turning to look at her. "Be careful. There are still too many unanswered questions about who did this. I don't want you to get hurt."

"I will." She gave him a small smile, but her insides were somersaulting over his concern for her.

CHAPTER SIX

She held still until she heard the outside door close then jumped up. "He believes me!" She'd waited so many years to hear him say those words and he finally had. Her heart pounded now that she allowed herself to revel in his support. Cole Hatcher believed she had nothing to do with the fire. If he believed her about this one, then he would soon realize she hadn't started the Orson fire.

She fairly skipped to the front desk as a guest approached. After sending a message to Rachel about the guest's husband's birthday, Lacey sat in front of her computer to approve the payroll. But she couldn't concentrate. If Cole believed her, there may be hope for them yet.

The question was why? Why did he believe her on this fire but hadn't when they were younger? What was different? She grinned. He was physically a hunk now, but beyond that he'd matured and so had she. The old Lacey would have jumped into his arms and told him to take her home with him.

A piece of her still wanted him to, but she was afraid. That's why she'd put him off. If he really wanted to see if there was a future for them, he would return. If he didn't, she'd be upset, but better that than being devastated…again. Now that her head was satisfied he supported her, her heart was afraid to trust him fully.

"Excuse me, I'm here for an interview."

She snapped her head around at the sound of another man's voice. How could she have been so engrossed in her thoughts not to hear him come in. "Hello. I'll be there in a minute."

She picked up the interview list then glanced at the clock. She must not have seen Mr. McKade leave while she was with Cole. "Are you Mr. Palmera?"

At the man's nod, she smiled. "Have a seat and I'll be right with you."

As the man strode to a lobby chair, she relaxed that he'd done as she suggested. Quickly, she headed for Kendra's office to let her know her next candidate was waiting. After knocking, and being bid to enter, she opened the door and hesitated. Mr. McKade stood behind the chair facing Kendra.

Kendra nodded toward the man. "Lacey, meet one of our new security guards. Hunter says he can start as early as tomorrow. Could you get him the necessary paperwork?"

"Of course." She tried to smile but couldn't. There was something about the man that bothered her, yet he'd been given Kendra's approval. What second chance could he possibly need?

He offered his hand. "I look forward to working with you, Lacey."

She looked past him at Kendra, who waved her hand in dismissal. He couldn't be that bad if Kendra hired him. She mustered a kind smile. "I look forward to having you here. We definitely need someone who can protect this place. If you could come this way?"

He opened his arm to indicate that she precede him, so she did, looking back once to be sure he followed. The man moved too quietly. Then again that could be a good thing in his line of work.

Getting him settled in the back room, she left him to his forms. What would Cole think about the man working at Poker Flat? On the other hand, it shouldn't even be a concern. Cole didn't work here, she did.

She returned to her computer to focus on payroll. No one would understand if they weren't paid because she was mooning over Cole. After getting the payroll approved, she printed out one more form to give to Hunter.

As she stepped into the staff room, he picked his hat up off the table and slammed it back on, but not before she noticed the scar that marred the back of his head, no hair growing from the healed skin.

Understanding for their new employee relaxed her. One reason Kendra hired the man had just become obvious. With a new appreciation for him, she settled in to making him feel welcome.

~~~~~

Cole couldn't find Billy, so he caught a ride with one of the guests, who was picking up his wife after her trail ride was over. The naked man had a large belly and joked his wife only tried the ride to make googly eyes at the resort manager. He, on the other hand, didn't plan to risk his balls for such a trivial pursuit.

Cole bit the inside of his mouth to keep from laughing. The man had a point. After all, his wife had to be old enough to be Wade's mother.

As they approached the barn, a very curvaceous woman with fake breasts and legs longer than an ostrich talked with Wade, her hand on his arm as she flirted, proving her husband right. When they came to a stop, the man stepped out of his cart and slapped the woman on her bare ass.

Her yelp was followed by her switching her attention to the older man and linking her arm with his.

Cole shook his head as the two entered the cart and drove back to the other side of the resort. He watched them go then looked at Wade, who wore a fake smile that didn't reach his eyes. Cole laughed. "It's safe now. You can stop smiling."

Wade rubbed his hands down his face. "That was a very long half-hour ride."

"You mean an hour-long thirty minutes?"

Wade smirked. "More like two hours. I know it's all harmless, but every once in a while I want to drop the fact that Kendra owns a Smith and Wesson 9mm and knows how to use it into the conversation."

Cole slapped him on the back. "I understand. I once had an elderly lady who called 9-1-1 once a week like clockwork because she 'couldn't breathe'. We finally figured out that she just wanted to ogle the firefighters, so we made a deal with her. We told her we would stop by once a week when we made a grocery run for the station if she promised not to call 9-1-1 unless it was a true emergency."

Wade raised a brow. "Did she agree?"

"Yes, she did. She would tell her friends that her boyfriends were coming over and make them leave. We only stayed for about fifteen minutes, but it made her week." Cole couldn't help smiling as he remembered her joy at seeing them.

"How old is she?"

He shook his head. "She passed away the summer before last. Ironically, when she did have a heart attack, she didn't realize it and never called 9-1-1. Every firefighter in our department insisted on going to her funeral. My chief told us we had to have a crew in gear with the truck there in case we got a call. She would have loved to have seen that."

"I'll have to remember that story next time my patience is at an end." Wade patted Ace and moved him inside. "So what brings you back to Poker Flat?"

Cole shrugged and leaned against a stall. "I wanted to find out if you had any word about the break-in."

Wade closed the stall door and stared at him. "You wanted to see Lacey again."

Shit, was he that transparent? "Yeah, I wanted to make sure she was okay and that the thieves didn't get a look at her."

"It was dark and she was at her house. The thieves didn't even know she was the one who saw them."

Cole relaxed. "Do you think the theft and the fire are linked?"

"No idea." Wade sat on a plastic chair and leaned it back on its legs until his shoulders hit the barn wall. "Not my job to figure that out."

"Who called 9-1-1?"

"Kendra." Wade folded his arms across his chest. "She usually works late, as in one or two in the morning. She used to be a professional poker player called The Night Owl, if you hadn't heard. She'd just left her office when she heard an explosion. When she reached the end of the hall, she saw the flames and called."

"Wow, that had to have been a shock." Cole squinted at the wall, picturing the scene. "So what happened next?"

"She called me and I came over to get her. Meanwhile she called all the staff on the grounds. Selma immediately went to the kitchen and Kendra and I came over here to make sure the horses remained safe."

"What about Lacey, Billy, your bartender and the waitress?"

Wade studied him. "Are you interrogating me?"

Shit, he'd gone too far. "No, no. Just curious. I rarely get to hear about what happened *before* I arrive to a fire." He shrugged. "Never mind. You don't have to tell me. I imagine you'd rather forget the whole thing."

Wade stood, looking just past him. "You probably don't want to move."

"What?" Cole turned around to see what the problem was only to stop at the sound of ripping material. "What the hell?" He looked into the innocent brown eyes of Daisy, his t-shirt firmly clenched between her teeth.

"I told you not to move." Wade chuckled as he walked over. "Here. The best way to do this is to slip out of your shirt and I can usually get her to open with some celery."

"Right." Cole did as Wade suggested then stood back and watched the man try to coax the big horse into relinquishing his clothing. "Aren't your guests bothered by her little habit?"

"No." Wade grinned. "Why would they be? They don't wear clothes."

Cole covered his eyes with his hand. Of course. He watched as Wade attempted to reason with the horse, but Daisy didn't care.

"You must smell pretty good because she really likes your shirt."

"Did you know she had this habit before you bought her?" Cole meandered along the other stalls.

"Yup. That's why I got her and Sage for such a great price."

Cole looked back at Wade. "Why did you get a good price on Sage?"

"Because he wouldn't budge without Daisy."

Wow, the fact the resort was for nudists may be the most normal part about the place. The staff and animals even had strange backgrounds. He stopped in front of one of the empty stalls. "Uh Wade, I think you might have a problem."

"You mean besides owing you a shirt?" Wade strode over and Cole pointed to the man lying on the concrete of the empty stall.

"Do you think he's dead?"

Wade sighed. "No, but he might as well be. That's Billy. He passed out."

Cole studied the clothing of the man lying on his side, his face toward the back wall. "But he just gave me a ride down not two hours ago."

Wade frowned. "He was probably half in the bag by then. We thought he was doing better, but he isn't. I haven't said anything to Kendra yet, but she may need to make a tough decision."

"Why doesn't he go to his casita when he's drunk?"

"He says it makes him claustrophobic. But I think it only feels that way to him when he drinks. He used to pass out in the rub down station, but I made him find an empty stall so the guests wouldn't see him."

Cole put a few pieces of information together. "So that's why he didn't hear the sirens when we pulled up the night of the fire."

Wade leaned on the half door of the stall. "No way he heard the commotion. He was so drunk that night he never made it to a stall. Kendra and I found him lying in the middle of the barn. She wasn't happy, but she had other things to worry about. I moved him into my office in case the barn caught fire."

"He's one lucky man."

Wade gave him a look he couldn't quite decipher.

"Everyone who works for Kendra is lucky."

Cole winked. "Some luckier than others."

A slow smile grew on Wade's face. "Got that right."

The sound of a golf cart's wheels crunching on the gravel outside had them both moving to the entrance of the barn. In the parking area, Lacey dropped off a couple nudists.

She spoke to Wade. "Mr. and Mrs. Irving would like to see the stagecoach." Then her gaze found his for a moment before she dropped it, giving his naked chest a thorough inspection. She took a deep breath then snapped her head around and turned the cart.

Wade chuckled, before lowering his voice. "So are you trying your luck again with Lacey?"

Cole sighed. "I'd like to, but she doesn't seem to be open to that right now." And it made him want to push it more. He was on edge, as if they had lost too much time already. What if he'd disobeyed his parents back then? Would Lacey and he still be together?

The nudists walked away toward the burn site, an ugly black mound on the otherwise pristine resort. It reminded him of the black mark on his otherwise perfect relationship with Lacey.

"Before you go down that path, you better be absolutely sure you're going to stay on it." Wade's grin disappeared. "Lacey isn't the type to take you back into her life unless she's fully committed. That girl puts her heart into everything she does and I know a lot of people around here who wouldn't be happy with you if you broke it again."

Cole shifted uncomfortably. Wade had a good point. If he planned to pursue her, this time he had to accept her for who she was, even that she had set the fire in Orson, but everything in him said she didn't start this one. Could he live with that? He needed to be absolutely sure this was the right course of action for both—

The ringing of his cellphone cut off his thought. He walked away for privacy as he listened to his contact at the Humane Society. His friend there always called him first when they found a horse that needed rescuing.

"Yes, I'll take her. Don't let anyone near her unless they are a certified vet. I'm on my way." He ended the call and walked toward the front of the barn where Wade put away tack.

"Bad news?"

"Yeah, I've got to go save a horse. Good thing you bought four. I'm going to need some of those funds to bring this one back."

"If you don't mind my asking, what are you saving it from?"

"Abuse. Purposeful, violent abuse." He couldn't help his hands forming fists. Abused horses always made him want to beat their owners to a pulp and this time it had been a fucking drunk who had done it. It would be his pleasure to testify at that trial.

"Hey." Wade's hand on his shoulder released him from his black thoughts for a moment. "As soon as the detective finds out how the fire started, I'll bring those horses here, so you don't need to care for them. Good luck with this new one."

Cole forced his jaw to work. "Thanks."

Wade nodded and let go. "What's the horse's name?"

"Angel." Rage filled his blood at the irony and he stalked away.

~~~~~~

Lacey woke with a start, her heart beating faster than a roadrunner could run. Glancing at her clock, she placed her hand on her chest. 3:48 a.m. At least her nightmares were occurring later every morning. That had to be a good sign. It had been five days since the first one. Maybe in another week she'd be able to sleep through the night.

They had changed again. Now Cole looked for her in the burning mass with no fire gear. Instead he wore his jeans, hat and no shirt like she'd seen him a couple days ago at the barn. She'd sensed he'd put on a lot of muscle, but the size of his pectoral muscles and the ripples of his abdomen had stayed with her all day, creating a readiness in her core that ached. Never would she have imagined he'd look so hard.

But watching Cole being buried in fiery rubble was taking its toll on her heart, not to mention her ability to concentrate during the day. Not seeing him yesterday didn't help. For all she knew, he could have been trapped in a burning building somewhere.

Shaking off the fear that came with her dream, she rose and donned her robe. She wouldn't even try to go back to sleep. She couldn't arrive at work for another couple hours so she'd get a head start at home.

She padded into the kitchen, turned on the light and started the coffeemaker. She could take her laptop outside, but with the new security guard roaming the premises, she wasn't willing to be seen in her jammies, even if they were Victoria's Secret sleepwear. Besides, the low temperature was supposed to be in the high fifties and that was a bit too cold for her.

Now where had she placed her laptop last night when she'd woken? Not seeing it in her little living room, she moved back into her bedroom. The room was dark and she paused a moment to enjoy the view of the setting moon. The bright-orange slice looked as if it would cut into the main building.

Out of habit, albeit a new one, she scanned the grounds around the building. Nothing moved. It was a quiet night as it had been all week. Moving to where her lamp sat next to the bed, she paused. Was that Hunter? She stepped up to her south facing window. "Oh my gosh."

There were three people huddled around a golf cart parked near the fork in the dirt road that entered the resort. They could very well be guests, but since Poker Flat now had a security guard, it couldn't hurt to be safe. She picked up her phone, which she kept next to her bed.

"What is it?"

So much for pleasantries. "Hunter, this is Lacey. There are three people by a golf cart at the fork. They could be guests, but I thought I should tell you."

"Got it. Don't call me. I'll let you know."

The phone went silent. She stared at it, not sure if he'd relieved her worry or added to it. She moved her gaze back to the window and watched. The people were only silhouettes to her, but if she squinted it looked like they wore clothes. She closed her eyes and reopened them. She couldn't be sure.

One sat in the golf cart like he would drive it away but the other two stood in front of it. If they were having an argument, that would keep them there until Hunter arrived. Lacey scanned the road toward the barn looking for him, but she couldn't see anything yet. She could see more if she stepped out her front door, but she wasn't that brave.

She looked back toward the cart. "Oh no." They all climbed in and the cart headed down the road toward the bridge and the exit. She watched it until it disappeared. She couldn't think of a single reason why three guests would be headed to the garage at this time of night. She looked toward the barn, but there was still no sign of the security guard. She had to let him know where they had gone.

She turned on the light and dialed. "Sugar." She exited before she pressed the final number. He said not to call. Something about Hunter made her hesitant to ignore what he said. She turned the light off again and waited for her eyes to adjust. She scanned the road and couldn't see a thing. What if Hunter was in trouble?

The buzz of her phone made her squeal. Breathless, she answered it. "Yes?"

"I've got the thieves. Call 9-1-1." Again the phone went silent.

She didn't hesitate. She called and let the dispatcher know what the emergency was. Once the woman had dispatched a deputy sheriff, Lacey exited the call. There was no way Hunter would be able to keep three men in line. Quickly, she dialed Wade's number. It sent her straight to his voice mailbox. More nervous by the minute, she called Kendra's phone. It also went to voice mail. Since when did those two both turn off their phones?

She wanted to call Cole, but that was crazy. She had no idea where he lived and he might even be working a fire. Just because he walked back into her life didn't mean he would stay nor that she could depend on him. She looked out her window again. Wherever Hunter had the thieves, it wasn't where she could see them. Then again, they couldn't see her.

Dropping her pajama bottoms and robe, she pulled on a pair of sweatpants and a sweatshirt and slipped on her flip-flops. Before she lost her courage, she grabbed up her phone and opened her front door. She stopped. The sliver of moon had half set behind the main building already. Taking her gaze from the pretty sight, she scanned the road again. Confident there was no one out there, she ran for Kendra's two-story house.

She focused on the ground the entire way, avoiding cacti and hopefully the late-night critters like rattlesnakes. When she made it to the door, she banged hard and stopped. She listened for sounds inside then banged hard again.

The door flew open and she was yanked inside the dark house.

"What are you doing?" Wade's voice made it clear he was angry even if she couldn't quite make out his features.

"I called, but both your phones went to voice mail. It's the thieves." She still panted a little and tried to catch her breath.

He grabbed her shoulders.

"The thieves? Where?"

"Hunter has them. He has three. I called 9-1-1 but I don't know where he is, and it could take them a half hour to get here. What if they overpower him?"

"Shit. Okay. Do you know where he caught them?"

"It was somewhere between the fork and the road up the other side of the canyon." Her heart slowed to a more normal rate. All these after-dark activities plus her nightmares had her overreacting, she was sure.

"Let me get dressed and I'll drop you off at your casita on my way to find Hunter." Wade let go of her and strode away in the dark.

It hadn't even occurred to her he might sleep naked. Duh. At least it was too dark to see. The last thing she wanted to be looking at was her boss's fiancé's parts no matter how hot he was because Kendra would *not* be happy.

Within minutes Wade was back in a t-shirt, jeans and boots. "Let's go."

As he drove her to her home, she quickly relayed what little Hunter said. When they reached her door, Wade put his hand on her arm. "You did good, Lacey. Now go inside, lock your door, and don't leave until you hear from me, okay?"

She nodded then jumped out and let herself in. Quickly, she turned and locked the door. She hadn't even thought to lock it while she ran to Kendra's. That wasn't very smart. She scanned the main area of her home. Luckily, nothing was amiss and she breathed a relieved sigh. She dropped her phone on the table and strolled into her bedroom to switch her flip-flops for her bunny slippers.

Returning to the kitchen, she pulled a cup out of the cupboard to pour herself some coffee.

She stepped toward the coffeemaker and froze at the napkin sitting next to it. A message was written in blue ink, the pen, one of her own, lay next to it.

IT WAS YOU.

She dropped the cup and it shattered on the tile floor. Backing up, she clasped both hands over her heart. Oh gosh, oh gosh. She shivered even as her body began to sweat. The thieves knew she'd seen them! Did one get away? Was Hunter hurt?

She had to tell Wade, Kendra, the sheriff's department, everyone right away. Darn.

Cole, I wish you were here.

CHAPTER SEVEN

At the sound of his phone vibrating, Cole glanced at the clock. Shit, it was only five in the morning. It was his last day off before going back on shift and he'd been up half the night with Angel. He checked the number and quickly answered. "Yeah."

"There's been another break-in at the nudist resort and things are getting dicey." Sean's voice was loud against the quiet morning. "You want to meet me over there?"

His gut tensed as he sat up. "Sure."

"Good. I'm heading over in about fifteen."

"Got it." Cole wished like hell he'd asked Lacey for her number. Was she okay? He could call the main number. She usually answered that, unless she was hurt. The thought had him jumping out of bed. What the fuck did "dicey" mean?

Anxious to see if Lacey was okay with his own eyes, he was dressed and in his truck in three minutes. He sped out of the driveway, hoping no police were on Carefree Highway and that his grandparents could figure out the note he left about Angel. He'd call as soon as he found out if Lacey was okay.

Ahead of him the sky was a pale pink, the sunrise still an hour away. Was Lacey even awake? Probably. She'd always been an early riser. He should have asked Sean what had happened, but he didn't want to push him. He should tell the detective his real relationship with Lacey.

At the nondescript dirt road with no sign, he turned off Carefree Highway, gripping the wheel tighter. If someone had been hurt, Sean would have said something. He would have said there was an accident or a shooting or— "Fuck."

Red and blue flashes of light peppered the desert landscape.

He pressed the gas pedal harder, sending up a cloud of dust to rival a haboob. He didn't care. His gut twisted with worry and the only way to relieve it was to see Lacey. Finally reaching the sign for Poker Flat, he fishtailed as he took the left too fast.

At the three-walled garage, Cole turned in and parked. No other car was there, which meant Sean hadn't arrived yet. Shit. Cole stepped out into the cool air and walked to the sheriff department car parked at the wooden boundary. No one was in it.

Looking across the ravine, he could see the lobby area was lit up. What had happened?

The sound of a vehicle coming down the road had him turning. Sean pulled into the garage in his unmarked car. Cole strode toward him, not willing to wait another minute.

As Sean exited his vehicle, Cole entered the covered area. "Is anyone hurt?"

Sean raised a brow. "Good morning to you, too."

Cole took a deep breath. "Sorry. You said it had become dicey. Is someone hurt?"

Sean shook his head. "Not yet."

The momentary relief Cole experienced disappeared like a frightened gecko. "What do you mean?"

"Walk with me and I'll explain. The owner is coming to pick us up. We might as well meet her at the barrier."

He nodded, swallowing the curse he'd been about to utter.

As Sean explained what happened, Cole's fear mingled with frustration until he couldn't keep quiet. "Someone was in her home?"

"Yes. Not for long though. I'm hoping I can find out who it was from the other three when I interrogate them."

Cole fisted his hands. "What about police protection? Will the sheriff's office provide that?"

"I doubt it." Sean pointed to a tan golf cart crossing the bridge over the stream. "Here she comes. The sheriff's office doesn't want to deal with this resort at all. Why do you think I was assigned to investigate the fire? They certainly aren't going to see the note as a threat."

"Not a threat?" His voice rose substantially and the detective looked at him shrewdly.

"I asked you to come as a professional courtesy and with the hope you might discover more from the staff. The firefighter is always the hero. But if you can't keep your cool, you're welcome to leave."

Cole gritted his teeth and simply nodded. He wasn't sure he could keep his voice down at the moment.

Luckily, Kendra Lowe pulled up. She gave him a questioning look then spoke to Sean. "The deputy sheriff is waiting for you. He said he has to get to court for a vehicle citation hearing." That she wasn't happy with the man's excuse for leaving was clear.

Cole climbed on the back of the cart, his anxiety rising over Lacey's safety. Shit, she had to be scared as hell. He ignored the passing beauty of the resort on the way down the canyon wall and instead focused on the woman he loved, had always loved.

Dumping her had to have been the dumbest thing he'd ever done, but he'd been young and his parents didn't want a criminal associated with their ranch. He'd planned to track her down when the cause of the fire had been determined accidental, but his parents told him her family's close relationship with the town manager had caused the charges to be dropped. There was no clear proof she was innocent.

So he'd moved on with his life, burying his love for her deep in his heart, never understanding why no other woman was the right one for him. Now that he'd found her again, the old feelings had taken over his every waking moment along with new, more mature emotions. There was no way he'd lose her again. Like she'd said the other day, he needed to stand by her no matter what, even if she had started the fire in Orson.

That he could lose her permanently scared the shit out of him. Somehow, he had to keep her safe.

The cart slowed as they approached the main building. Before the vehicle stopped, he jumped off and ran for the front doors of the resort. When he entered, he saw her at once. Ignoring the fact she was surrounded by staff and a deputy sheriff, he strode forward.

Lacey's gaze swung to him and her tense features relaxed into relief.

It was all he needed to see. Stepping between everyone, he stopped in front of her. "Lacey?"

"Cole." Fear and need ran across her features, before a tiny tear appeared at the corner of one eye.

He wrapped his arms around her and leaned his chin on her head. The feel of her in his arms tilted his world upright again. Memories of holding her close sped through his mind as he inhaled her fresh scent. A basic instinct welled up from within his heart and permeated his brain. *Forever.*

A clearing of a throat reminded him where he was, but he didn't care. He pulled back a bit and lifted Lacey's chin to look into her watery brown eyes, the light-gold flecks sparkled against her tears. He kept his voice low and soft, for her ears only. "I'm here. I won't let anything happen to you."

She smiled tentatively.

"Cole, is there something you want to tell me?" Sean's voice held serious sarcasm.

He released Lacey partly, keeping one arm wrapped around her waist and addressed the detective. "Yes. You may want to research the financials of Price Construction."

Sean raised an eyebrow before turning toward the deputy, who looked happy they'd arrived.

"Thank you for coming." Lacey's soft voice had him gazing at her again.

There was so much he wanted to tell her, but his fear of rejection cut off the words he really wanted to say. "I had to." *Tell her. What do you have to lose?* "You—"

"Whoa and who is this hunk of a cowboy?" The strange woman's voice interrupted him and irritation tensed his muscles. He looked up to tell her to get lost, but Lacey surprised him by stepping in front of him.

LEXI POST

"His name is Cole Hatcher. He was the firefighter in charge the other night. I've known him for years."

If he didn't know better, he'd say his sweet Lacey was protecting him. He took a closer look at the woman. She had the smooth skin of a first generation Mexican American with an elegant face. Her long black hair and dark-brown eyes would cause her enough attention from the opposite sex, but coupled with a significant bustline, tiny waist and curvy hips that ended in long, gorgeous legs, she would be irresistible…if a man was into all that.

The siren's eyes widened as she looked at Lacey. Then she nodded and held out her hand. "Hi, I'm Adriana, the bartender here. We haven't met yet, but I will tell you if you hurt this woman, I will personally shoot you."

It took his brain a minute to register what she said as she said it with a sultry smile, as if she wanted to bed him, not kill him. He blinked then nodded seriously. "Warning filed."

She flipped her hair back over her shoulder and moved toward the deputy, who appeared to be trying to cut short his conversation with Kendra. Bemused, Cole watched as the bartender sidled up to the man and offered to take him back to his car.

Lacey slapped his chest. "Cole Hatcher, what are you staring at?"

He moved his gaze to her. "The most beautiful and courageous woman I know." He touched her cheek, unable to resist. Now that he'd touched her, held her, he didn't want to stop.

As he hoped, she forgot about the bartender and focused on him. "I wasn't very courageous. Shoot, I completely freaked out."

He smiled as his heart warmed. She still wouldn't swear, a trait that had always triggered his protective instincts and it did the

106

same now…when she actually needed it. He took her in his arms again. "You had every right to be scared, but not anymore. I'm not leaving your side until they catch whoever is doing this."

Her eyes widened. "But you can't do that. You have a job and a ranch to run."

"There's nothing more important than you." His heart skipped as she looked away. Shit, had he really hurt her that much? He was an ass to make her so uncomfortable now. "I can always call my grandfather and tell him what to do with Angel."

"Angel?"

He congratulated himself on distracting her. "Yes, Angel. She's a white Arabian. I just got her in."

"Where did you buy her from?"

He loved that she stayed in the circle of his arms as they talked, despite all the commotion around them. "I didn't buy her. I save abused, neglected and hurt horses that owners don't want. Or at least I try to. Not all make it."

Her face softened. "Oh Cole. That's so amazing. What's wrong with Angel?"

He tried not to tense around her, but his stomach tightened at the image of Angel as he'd last seen her. "She has been flayed brutally by a drunk bastard, but the vet says she has a sixty percent chance of making it and I'm betting on those odds."

"How could someone do such a thing?"

He shook his head. The abuse cases were the worst because the damage was purposeful and nasty. "I don't know. But I'll do everything I can to save her. Who knows, someday she may end up here."

"Here? Why here?"

"Didn't Wade tell you? He bought four of my horses and plans to buy more."

Lacey frowned. "I haven't seen any paperwork. Why would he hide that from me?"

He squeezed her a little to gain her attention. "We haven't done any yet. Wade wanted to wait until they caught whoever started the fire and who broke in."

Lacey's face paled. "I saw them and they know I did. There were four in all, but Hunter only caught three. He didn't know there was a fourth until I called him."

Cole looked over her head at the man in black leaning against one of the beams that held up the massive roof, his arms crossed over his chest, his black cowboy hat shading his eyes. "Mind if we go talk to him?"

She shrugged. "You're welcome to try, but good luck. He doesn't say much."

As much as he would prefer to stay there all day with Lacey in his arms, his need to protect her was stronger. Removing one arm from around her, he walked her over to where Hunter stood, pretending not to watch the proceedings, but it was evident he did.

Cole held out his hand. "Hunter, I'm Cole Hatcher."

The man grasped his hand and shook, but didn't say a word.

"Lacey tells me you caught three of the four men who broke in. Do you think the fourth is still here hiding?"

Hunter shook his head. "Found tracks. He's long gone."

That pronouncement brought him some relief, but it didn't mean the trespasser would stay away.

Lacey studied Hunter. "I'm so glad you weren't hurt. I mean, there were three of them. I saw them."

Hunter looked over her head. "Kids."

"Kids?" Cole frowned. "You mean teenagers?"

Again, Hunter shook his head. "College."

Hmm, Desert Rim University was nearby, or as nearby as anything could be. He couldn't think of any other college close enough for students to make the trek out to Poker Flat. "Were they just trespassing or did they do damage?"

Hunter motioned with his head toward the front. "They were stealing a golf cart."

Lacey looked up at Cole in puzzlement before her face flushed with excitement. "That means they had a big enough vehicle nearby to put the golf cart in. That's how the fourth one got away."

He smiled at her. If only she'd seen the fourth one in her house. Then she could tell a sketch artist what the guy looked like.

He forced himself to move his gaze to Hunter. "Thank you. Both of us are breathing easier now." The man made the slightest movement with his shoulders as if to shrug. He was definitely different, but he'd caught three college boys and Cole didn't doubt that hadn't been easy.

Sean joined them. "I'm going to need to take statements from everyone who was involved last night before I interrogate the suspects. I'll start with you, Mr. McKade."

As Sean and Hunter moved down the hallway to Kendra's office, Lacey sighed. "Here we go again."

"Has Poker Flat always had so many issues?"

"It seems like it. Someone is always out to make trouble for us. I don't understand why they can't simply live and let live. Nudists are people like you and me, but lately it seems like they are even better. Oh no, I have to get to work. Kendra's good friends are coming today."

"Whoa, wait a minute. You've been through a harrowing night. Can't you have the day off?"

She put her hand on his chest, which he didn't mind at all.

"That would be nice, but no, we only have the staff we need to run the resort until Kendra is sure we can afford more. Besides, what am I supposed to do, sit at home thinking about what happened over and over again?"

"I can think of other things you could do." He winked, anxious to judge her reaction.

At her full-blown blush, hope kindled inside him.

"Cole, behave yourself."

"You say that to me at a nudist resort?" He feigned shock.

She smiled. "Now I have to get to work. The guests will be waking up soon and Buddy and Ginger will be arriving this morning. We need to get ready."

"Then I'll camp out in the lobby."

She stared at him as if he'd just turned into a giant dust devil. "Don't be ridiculous. It's daytime, the resort is full with guests and the staff are all here. I'll be fine. You have a horse that needs you. I don't."

He scowled at her final comment, not liking the way that sounded at all.

Lacey slapped him on the arm. "Oh please. Go take care of Angel. If you want, we can have dinner tonight. Okay?"

He grinned. "Okay." He wanted more than anything to give her a kiss, but a nude couple entered the lobby and he doubted Lacey would appreciate him doing that in front of them. Shit, he felt like he was walking over a nest of scorpions with her. One wrong step and he'd be struck. "I'll tell Sean I'm leaving." Even as he said the words, he could see Lacey pull herself into efficient receptionist mode though she wasn't behind her counter yet.

She lowered her voice. "See you tonight." After a quick smile to him, she moved off to greet the couple.

He watched for a moment, impressed with her professionalism despite preferring she kept her attention on him, but then he moved down the hallway toward Kendra's office. He had his own responsibilities to take care of before he went on shift tomorrow morning.

Halfway down the hall Hunter passed him. The man gave the smallest of nods and walked by. Cole wanted to dislike him, but he'd done his job well and there was something about him that reminded Cole of his horses, which made no sense.

Finding the office door open, he stepped in and cleared his throat.

Sean looked up from the notes he'd been making. "You're not going to believe this."

Cole strode in and took a seat opposite Sean. "What? What did Hunter tell you?"

Sean ran his hand across his buzz cut. "These students are from a fraternity and they are pledging. And of all the asinine things, part of the pledge is to steal something from this resort. Can you believe that?"

"What? That's nuts. What does this fraternity want? A house full of men with records?"

Sean shook his head.

"So what about Lacey?" He was crazy to ask but it was already obvious he had feelings for her and he was worried about what the frat boys might do to her.

"If you are so head over heels for her, why did you tell me she had been accused of starting the fire in Orson?"

He looked away. "I had to. It was information about someone on this resort that might be critical to the investigation. Is she a suspect?"

"Yes."

Cole felt his heart freeze in his chest. He couldn't believe it. There was a chance she'd simply been in the wrong place at the wrong time with the Orson fire, but Lacey wasn't stupid. This time, he was with her a hundred percent. "Why?"

Sean studied him. "If I tell you, you can't tell her. No, forget it."

His arm shot out faster than he could think and he grabbed Sean's shoulder. "Tell me. I promise to keep it to myself."

Sean stared him in the face and finally nodded. "Okay, the fire was started by a small campfire made outside with scraps the construction workers had thrown from the building, paper, plywood pieces, coffee cups, even candy wrappers. It's a wonder I didn't find a graham cracker box and marshmallow bag."

Guess he hadn't been that far off when he'd wondered that night if the guests would make s'mores. "So what does a campfire have to do with Lacey? I can honestly tell you she was never into camping."

"Someone had to build that little fire and then leave it burning unattended. It traveled through the construction debris outside and then into the building, following the path of combustibles. It took a while because it's new construction and once the fire made it to the building it hit fresh wood. As the fire burned, it melted a total of four five-gallon gas containers that were scattered about the place for the generator. All I have for identification purposes is Lacey Winters' sweater and a Tequila bottle, which I'm hoping has fingerprints."

"But these kids from the college, another staff person or even a guest could have started that campfire and not left anything behind." Cole didn't like the panic rising in his throat and made sure his voice didn't reveal it.

"True. Kendra and Wade have solid alibis, with each other, but since Kendra didn't have an unreasonable insurance amount on the new construction, she had nothing to gain and a lot to lose. Fires are not good for business. I will be talking to Billy, Rachel, Selma, Adriana and Lacey again today. Then I'll see what I can flesh out of those already taken into custody."

He didn't like the idea that Lacey would be interrogated again. He wanted to be here for her, but there was no way Sean would allow that and still give him information. "What about the construction company. If you're talking dollars, they had the most to gain."

"But a campfire? And none of them worked here on the weekend."

"And what a great way to hide the purpose of the fire. What I get stuck on is that you said someone had to let the fire burn unattended for a long while."

Sean nodded. "Yeah, I can see these college kids building one then leaving and not bothering to put it out. Still, I have to cover every possible avenue. At least we now know what the thefts have been about and can stop it." A gleam came into Sean's eyes and he relaxed back against his chair. "I'm thinking a major scare tactic is going to be needed to dissuade these frat boys."

Cole grinned. Sean was one of the easiest going guys on the force, but he was hardnosed when it came to stupidity. "What did you have in mind and how can I help?"

Sean tapped the pen on his pad. "I'm thinking a safety inspection on their frat house with a number of 'arrests' and a night in jail could work."

"Count me in."

"Good. But how much can I count on you with this fire investigation?"

That was a good question. "You can count on me to be truthful."

Sean stared at him a long time, before he nodded. "Good enough."

"I'm going to head out now. I have a horse in poor condition." Cole stood. "But I'm coming back this evening, so I'll keep my ear to the ground."

"Thanks, I appreciate it. On your way out, send Kendra in."

Cole gave Sean a quick nod and strode down the hall to the lobby. He told Kendra Sean wanted her then he looked for Lacey. She wasn't behind the desk, so he forced himself to leave. There was a good chance she was in back with the cook, making sure everything was ready for the coming day. She'd always been able to organize.

Setting his hat on his head, he walked outside as Billy pulled up, his smile wide. "Hey, cowboy, need a lift?"

"Perfect timing." He climbed in the golf cart.

Billy's hair was still wet and he smelled of cologne. It was hard to believe he was the same man passed out in the horse stall a couple days ago.

"Did you hears about all the ruckus?" Billy set the cart in motion, taking them down the road to the bridge.

"I did." He doubted Billy actually heard anything last night.

"Sure's nice having security here again. Makes it easier to sleeps at night."

Somehow, he doubted Billy had a hard time sleeping. "I think Detective Anderson will be putting a stop to any more vandalism by this particular crowd."

They rumbled across the bridge as Billy shook his head. "College kids. Never did understands what good all that schoolin' does 'em."

Cole swallowed a laugh, not willing to insult the old man. He was harmless and just trying to do his job between his drinks. Kendra was a much more patient boss than he could ever be. "Do you always work so early in the morning?"

Billy smacked the steering wheel. "You betcha. These nudists loves the sun so they gets here early, but that's okay, 'cause I gets off as soon as the sun goes down behind this ridge."

The cart crested the ravine ledge and Billy drove around the barrier. As they approached the garage, Cole noticed a small black pile against the north wall.

"Okay, here's you go. I gots to go gets Hunter now. He be movin' his stuff into Wade's old casita today."

Cole was glad the security guard would be settling in. It made the place safer for Lacey. "Thanks for the ride."

"Anytimes."

He shook his head as he watched Billy drive around the barrier and back over the ravine's edge. With characters like Billy and Adriana and even Kendra herself, Poker Flat had to be one of the strangest places in the whole country.

About to enter the garage, he changed his mind and walked to the north end of the steel structure where he'd noticed the black spot. Looking around the corner, he tensed. Not twenty feet away was what looked like a burned-out campfire. He walked to it and kicked the leftover debris. It was definitely a few days old. Fuck. It could have started a wildfire that would have traveled miles in this terrain.

Now this was something Sean should know about and it definitely had nothing to do with Lacey. Pulling out his phone, he strode to his truck.

"Hello, Sean? There's something up here by the guest garage that you should see."

CHAPTER EIGHT

Lacey looked at the clock for the fifth time in the last ten minutes. Frustrated with how slow time was moving, she pushed her chair away from the computer and stood.

"Something wrong, honey?"

Not aware anyone had approached the front desk, it took her a minute to compose herself before walking forward to respond to Ginger, Kendra's dear friend. "I'm sorry, I didn't see you there."

The older woman with bright, naturally orange hair smiled widely. She and her husband had been the reason Kendra had built Poker Flat in the first place. The last thing Lacey wanted to do was keep her waiting.

"Don't you worry none, sweetie. I imagine you were off daydreaming about that hunky cowboy in blue jeans I saw walking down the back hall yesterday."

Her cheeks warmed. Ginger had hit the spot. "To be truthful, I was daydreaming a little." She smiled wanly, not particularly happy about how anxious she was to have Cole coming for dinner. He was her weakness and despite eight years of separation, her heart was busy knocking down the hard-fought walls she'd constructed around it as it clamored to reach Cole.

"I don't blame you one bit." The woman chuckled. "I swear if he looked at me like he looked at you this morning, I'd have to think twice before turning back to Buddy."

Lacey shook her head. "Now, Ginger, I know for a fact nothing could take you away from your husband. You two were made for each other."

"And how do you know you two weren't made for each other as well?" Ginger smirked.

If she and Cole had been made for each other, would he have been so quick to abandon her? "I don't think so. We have a history and he's the one who ended it. I don't think I can trust him again."

"Did the bastard sleep around on you?"

It took Lacey a minute to register the older woman's words. "No! Cole would never be unfaithful."

"Well, if he didn't cheat on you, because I say once a cheater, always a cheater, then he deserves a second chance, right?"

She wanted to give him another chance. She really did, but she was so afraid of being hurt again and never being able to recover. She hadn't dated more than six years after him. If they tried again and he betrayed her… Her stomach tightened painfully at the thought.

Ginger reached across the counter and grasped her hand. "Sweetie, I'm not telling you what to do. Just giving you an outsider's perspective. It seems to me that Kendra built this place especially for second chances, but if you can't offer that, you don't have to. You do what's right for you."

She stared at the woman with teary eyes and nodded. "Thank you." Maybe Ginger was right. Maybe Cole did deserve a second chance. It wasn't like she was perfect either.

Ginger released her hand. "I'm happy to help."

Lacey wiped her eyes and smiled. "Now what can I do for you? You probably didn't come over here to advise me on my love life."

"No, I didn't know my expert advice would be needed." Ginger winked. "I came over here because Buddy was wondering if you had a volleyball net for the pool. He noticed the poles and hooks, but didn't know where to find it."

"Of course. The last one broke, but a new one came in yesterday. I haven't had a chance to unpack it yet. I'll be happy to bring it out for you."

"Lovely. Thank you, sweetie. I can see why Kendra depends so much on you. You are one efficient lady."

Ginger sauntered out the lobby doors and Lacey mused. The freckles on the woman's face and chest were all over her body and she could have cared less. That's what she liked about Poker Flat, everyone was welcome…everyone but thieves and arsonists.

Detective Anderson hadn't only asked her about the fire at Poker Flat, but also the one in Orson. Cole must have told him about it. She wanted to resent him, but that was just who he was. He always did what he was supposed to do, tell the truth, admit guilt, obey his parents, wear a condom.

She heated as a memory came with her last thought. They had unexpectedly been left alone together on her eighteenth birthday. Her mom ran out because she forgot birthday candles and needed to pick up a friend. Cole had immediately taken advantage of the situation, but hadn't brought a condom because he thought they'd be surrounded by twenty people all afternoon.

That was the first time he'd made her come with his tongue. She never forgot the excitement and titillating experience of sitting on the couch, her skirt up, her panties down and his tongue working her clit while his finger pumped into her with her mother and guests due to arrive within minutes.

Gosh, just the memory of that episode had her folds growing moist. They finished as her mother's car pulled into the driveway and he'd tried to kiss her. She'd turned her head and quickly dressed. He called her a scaredy cat for that move, but she'd been so sure her mom would be able to tell she'd just had an amazing orgasm, she was as nervous as a rabbit in a rattler's den.

If only Cole knew her like she had known him. If he did, he would have never believed she set the fire in Orson. But now he believed she hadn't set the fire at Poker Flat. Something changed. Could it be he finally realized she'd been innocent all along? If so, it opened up so many possibilities for them, throwing her back to a time when he loved her so much, he couldn't wait to have her to himself and unwrap her from her clothes. He'd loved her sexy lingerie and an image of his hard-on at seeing her in it had her body tingling.

Clasping her hands in front of her, she walked to the back room. She wasn't hungry, but chocolate had a certain soothing effect on her libido and memories of Cole certainly revved that up. Unwrapping a candy bar, she took a bite and glanced at the clock hanging on the wall.

She threw the candy wrapper in the trash and spotted the box with the volleyball net. Oh sugar, she forgot about getting that out to Buddy. Quickly, she pulled a box cutter out of a drawer and sliced through the package. In no time, she had the net out and left the office. She collided with Adriana as she entered the lobby.

"Hey, try to focus on where you're going, honey." Adriana carried a six pack of specialty beer.

"Sorry. I wasn't paying attention."

Adriana placed her hands on her hips, the six pack tipping dangerously. "Thinking about that cowboy I saw you with this morning?"

She shrugged. Better not to say anything.

"Look, that man is hotter than the inside of a car with black interior at midday on July fourth in Phoenix, but that doesn't mean he's right for you. Kendra told me he's the one who broke your heart but then I see you in his arms. What's with that?"

She looked away. It had been so easy to lean on Cole. "I was scared. He came to make sure I was safe." She returned her gaze to Adriana. "I can't just turn off the feelings I have for him." Why did she keep trying to explain how she felt when she didn't know herself?

"Listen, honey, here's my advice. Your body misses him. Take him to your place, fuck his brains out and then cut him loose. If you can't, then it's time to make him toe the line and I'd be happy to help you."

Lacey widened her eyes, caught speechless for a moment, then something about Adriana's smirk had sirens sounding in her head. She squinted her eyes at the bartender. "Don't you dare."

Adriana raised her sculpted eyebrows and bare shoulders. "What? All I said was that I'd help."

She pointed her finger at her friend. "I know how you set up that strip poker game with Wade and Kendra. I don't need your kind of help, thank you."

"Oh, come on girl. I could tie him up in a chair in your pretty little casita and you could have your way with him. After all, I hear cowboys like rope." She winked before turning toward the bar.

"What?"

Adriana sauntered away. "No worries, hon. I'll be sure to strip him first."

Lacey leaned back against the wall as the image of Cole tied naked to a chair appeared before her. The erotic vision had need coursing through her so hard her knees grew weak.

Anxiously, she fanned herself as she scowled at the large gathering room where Adriana disappeared. That woman needed to fall in love and see exactly how hard it could be. Even at the thought, Lacey relented. She hoped someday someone could make Adriana happy. There was a heart of gold beneath all that sex appeal, but it would take a tough hombre to run the gauntlet she'd put up around it.

Was that what she'd done? Made the path to her heart so complicated nothing Cole did would solve the maze she'd created? She wasn't like Adriana who enjoyed her one-night sex adventures. Lacey wanted a home with a man who believed in her. Maybe, down the road, even some children. Cole would make a great father. His integrity was impeccable, even if she'd ended up on the other side of it.

She glanced at the clock in the main gathering area. Maybe he wouldn't come.

Maybe Angel was worse off than he thought. An innocent horse being abused broke her heart. That Cole cared enough to make a place for such animals made the walls around her heart fall a little more. His parents had to have been furious. They were so proud of their horses' lineage. She could see them refusing to help him. He'd stood up to them for his horses. Why couldn't he have done the same for her?

Because he didn't want a relationship with an arsonist. It all came down to that. But would Cole want to try again if he still believed she'd started the Orson fire? He must have had a change of heart. That had to be why he kept trying to start their relationship again. Hope rekindled in her chest, burning any remaining defenses she had.

She pushed away from the wall, a new excitement bubbling inside. She hurried through the gathering room, the indoor bar, and outside to the pool area. Scanning the nudists lounging about, she spotted Buddy. He always wore a baseball cap because he was balding and didn't want to burn. The rest of him had a dark tan, like his wife.

Refusing to look toward the bar where she was sure Adriana would be smiling and winking at her, she brought the net over. "Here you go."

Buddy looked up from his book. "Ah Lacey, I knew we could count on you. Do you want to join us?"

She waved her finger at him. "Now you know I can't do that. I'm on the clock. All employees must be clothed while working."

He glanced over at his wife, who wore a look of "I told you so."

"I guess I lost that bet. Ginger said you wouldn't because you follow the rules, always."

She smiled at Ginger before nodding to Buddy. "That's right, and don't you forget it."

Buddy laughed and she turned away to return to the front desk. She waved at a few of the guests and answered one person's question, then entered the indoor bar. She stopped short.

Cole stood there, hat in hand, wearing a blue collared shirt, black hat, blue jeans and brown cowboy boots. The man in a t-shirt was a tease, but dressed up, he made her belly do somersaults.

"Hi, Lacey. Ready for dinner?"

She would prefer to go straight to dessert and simply have him, but that was out of the question. Adriana's suggestion flitted across her mind before she shook her head. "Wow, you look nice." She glanced down at her long beige skirt and yellow flowered top and felt downright dowdy. "I didn't know we were dressing up." She smirked. "Usually people don't wear clothes to dinner here."

He stepped closer, his woodsy scent flooding her with memories. "Where do you look?"

"What do you mean?" He glanced over her head and she turned. "You mean with the guests?"

"Yeah."

She turned back, ready to give him a set down, but he appeared honestly curious. She calmed down her immediate defense. "I look them in the eyes like I do with everyone. At first it was strange, everyone walking around naked, but now…" She shrugged. "I don't really notice anymore. It becomes the norm."

"I admit if you walked around naked, your eyes wouldn't be the only thing I'd look at."

Her body heated as his gaze focused on her.

"Do you still wear sexy lingerie beneath your clothes?" He blatantly stared at her chest and her nipples responded.

"Cole Hatcher, stop that."

His gaze moved to her eyes and he winked. "Are you hungry?"

The double entendre was not lost on her. The man was laying on the charm and she may be weakening, but she could set him back with the rest of them. "Yes, I am and I know for a fact Selma made her double cheese beef quesadillas today. They smell wonderful."

Cole's look of disappointment was perfect. She congratulated herself on keeping control of their conversation, and relationship, such as it was.

"Actually, I brought pizza."

She looked around but didn't see any. "You did?"

He motioned with his hat. "When you weren't at the front desk, I went into the back room, but I left it there when I couldn't find you. It's sausage and extra cheese."

"That's my favorite."

"I know." His smile faded. "I thought we could take it back to your casita. That way you wouldn't have to worry about the rest of the staff watching us have dinner."

She grimaced. "Yes, my new family can be a bit nosy."

"It *would* give us more privacy."

"Good point. No need for anyone to listen to our conversation."

Cole stepped closer. "Lacey, I want more than conversation with you."

His warm green eyes threatened to drown her. She could always count on Cole to be straightforward. He never had a hidden agenda. He always came right out and said what he wanted and now he wanted her. She swallowed hard, not sure she could handle that no matter how much her body wanted her to.

He touched her cheek, gently. "You know I'd never ask more of you than you are willing to give, right?"

His touch, so familiar, had her leaning toward him. She nodded. Cole was foremost a gentleman. There were many parts of him she could put her trust in. She just wasn't sure about giving him her heart again. That he had a good heart wasn't the question.

She stepped away, needing a little space. "How is Angel doing?"

"Better." He looked away, his face serious. "She seems to know we are trying to help her, but she's also afraid of us. If she had her way, she wouldn't let us in the stall with her at all. When we have to touch her, she shivers."

"Oh Cole. That's heartbreaking." If only Angel could understand how lucky she was to have Cole taking care of her.

One corner of his lips quirked up. "But I found her weakness."

"What's that?"

"Jellybeans. I have Elsa to thank for that. Wade will be bringing her here. I often keep jellybeans in my pocket for her and Angel sniffed them out. By the way, one of your Belgians, Daisy, likes them, too."

Lacey smiled. Cole's love of horses hadn't changed at all. It was another one of his qualities that pulled at her heart.

"Hmm. It seems all the ladies like jellybeans." He gave her a calculating grin. "Do you?"

"No, I'm afraid I don't. But I do like pizza that's not cold, hint, hint."

"Then let's go get it." Cole swept his hat to the side to allow her to lead then fell in step next to her.

His long stride, punctuated on the tile floor by his boots, was twice the length of hers. He used to tell her he liked that because she moved so quickly it was the only way he could keep up with her.

Everything about him reminded her of their past. All those pieces were good, perfect even, except the day he dumped her. Maybe she needed to forget about the old Cole and learn about the new one. That he believed in her was a huge difference between the two Coles. Obviously, something had changed.

With that plan in mind and a bit more confidence about having him over for dinner, she logged off her computer, let Kendra know she was done for the night, and brought Cole home.

~~~~~

Lacey popped the last bite of pizza into her mouth and sighed. "That was heaven. I haven't had pizza in over a month. Living here where everything is provided doesn't exactly induce me to leave much." She lifted one shoulder then reached for a napkin.

Cole caught her hand before she could pick it up. "Allow me." He brought her hand near his mouth and then proceeded to lick and suck each finger clean.

Her throat went dry and her limbs weakened, along with her resolve. She'd thought making him sit across from her would be safer, but it made looking at him over dinner that much easier.

More than his physical appearance had changed since she'd last seen him. His laughter was more relaxed now. He'd matured, become comfortable with himself, as if he didn't care what others thought anymore, something that had been very important to him when they were in high school. She definitely liked this new Cole.

Not that she was discounting the strong physical aspect of the man who sat there holding her hand, his tongue sweeping down one finger before taking that digit into his mouth. He'd rolled up his sleeves and the muscle in his forearm moved as he held her wrist, turning it slightly to better access her fingers.

Then he stroked his tongue up her palm and a sizzle of desire ran straight to her core. She pulled her hand back. "Thank you."

His gaze was warm. "My pleasure."

Oh gosh. He was pouring on the charm again and her fortifications were crumbling. Adriana's words flitted through her mind. *Your body misses him. Take him to your place, fuck his brains out and then cut him loose.* But that wasn't who she was. The fact was, she still loved him deeply despite the hurt he'd caused. She *wanted* to give him another chance.

"Lacey, what's wrong?" Cole's face showed so much concern, she couldn't hide her fears anymore.

"I'm afraid."

He immediately rose and grabbed the chair next to her, moving it to face her before he took her hands in his. "I'm here. I won't let anyone harm you, I promise."

That wasn't what she meant, but his sincerity blew away her final defense. "I believe you. I feel completely secure with you here. I know no one could hurt me…except you."

Hurt flitted across his face so quickly, she could have imagined it.

"I can't undo the past. I wish I could." He hesitated, as if trying to find the right words. "Now that you've come into my life again, you're all I think about. We had something special. I think we still can have that."

She opened her mouth but he released one of her hands to put his finger against her lips.

"You probably have a million reasons why we shouldn't try again, and I probably have a million to argue against you, but the bottom line is, I love you. And my gut tells me I'll never love anyone like I love you."

Hope, that illusive human frailty, took root in her heart and began to grow.

He squeezed her hand gently. "I don't expect anything from you right now. All I ask is that you give us a second chance."

A second chance, like she'd been given at Poker Flat. Her mind said it was only fair. Her heart clamored for her to agree. Her body yearned to feel him inside her again. She couldn't deny it any longer. "I guess we could—"

Cole pulled her up into his arms, taking her breath away. He cupped the back of her head and lowered his lips to within an inch of hers. "You have the most beautiful heart."

Her breath hitched and then his lips were upon hers, firm against her own, urging her to open to him. She gave him access and his tongue swept into her mouth, exploring like he'd never kissed her before.

She grasped his broad shoulders, feeling so tiny against the new Cole, his tongue making her toes curl in her cowboy boots. Tentatively, she pushed her tongue into his mouth and he throttled back, allowing her to explore, until he moaned.

The sound of his need made her more confident. The man was hot and she wanted him. She moved her hands to around his neck and pressed her breasts against his massive chest. He was so big, he enveloped her as if he could protect her from the world. She'd always loved that he was so much taller, but now, every feminine nerve ending focused on being loved by him.

Cole broke away, his breathing heavy. "Bedroom?"

She nodded toward her left.

He scooped her up and carried her with ease, something he hadn't been capable of before. Just the thought of his hard chest and what she'd seen of it at the barn had her licking her lips.

Cole set her on the side of the bed and knelt at her feet. Like a prince checking to see if the glass slipper fit, he carefully pulled off her boots. Then he rolled down her knee socks and draped them on the boots.

He took one bare foot into his large hand and kissed the arch. A tingle of anticipation wove its way up her leg. This was definitely a new Cole. There had been times when they'd been so anxious to have sex that no clothes came off at all. They'd simply been pushed aside.

He held her foot with one hand, and ran his other up her calf, across her knee, and over her thigh. But he didn't touch her where she wanted to be touched. Instead, he repeated the same actions with her other foot and leg. She held her breath as his hand moved up her other thigh, but he didn't go any farther.

When he pulled his hand from beneath her skirt, he brought his palm to his nose. "Fresh Linen. I love that scent."

He remembered. His words fed her heart even as his gaze fed her soul. Gosh, she'd missed him.

Still kneeling, he unbuttoned the first button of her shirt. When she moved her hands to help, he caught them in his own. "Let me."

The green of his eyes was darker, the blue flecks more pronounced and she caught her breath before agreeing. Unhurriedly, he unbuttoned each button, pulling the blouse from beneath her waistband to tackle the last two. Then, as if opening a precious present, he spread her shirt apart and stilled.

He'd asked if she still wore racy lingerie. It was her one personal pleasure. His eyes riveted to the pure-white mesh bra that concealed nothing. Even as he stared, her nipples pushed against the fine fibers, teasing her more.

Cole swallowed hard. "Lacey, you don't know what you do to me."

"Then show me." Her folds moistened just thinking about what his naked body would look like now.

His gaze snapped to hers and he grinned as he shook his head. "Not yet, Racy Lacey. I want to enjoy every second of your unveiling."

She pouted and he traced his finger over her lip. Unable to resist, she stuck her tongue out and licked.

He shuddered and pulled his hand away.

He had to be hard and she desperately wanted to see. But Cole was too intent on her as he pushed her shirt over her shoulders and pulled it away, throwing it over her dressing table stool.

"Lean back and lift your hips."

She grinned. "My pleasure."

He coughed at her tease, but didn't let it stop him from pulling the elastic waist of her skirt down past her hips and over her feet. This time he dropped the skirt as he stared at her thong panties. "Jesus, Lacey, you'd tempt a saint."

"I don't want a saint, Cole. I want you."

He stared at her as if her invitation were too good to be true. Taking her face in his hands, he kissed her gently, his mouth on hers so tender, she felt revered. When he leaned his forehead on hers and breathed deeply, she understood he was trying to stay in control. That he did this for her warmed her soul.

She touched his face. She could see the young man he had been beneath the mature person he was now and again wondered at his transformation. "I want to see you."

He leaned back. "I'm right here."

"No, I mean without your clothes." She ruffled what hair he had, surprised by its softness.

"As you wish." He unbuttoned his dress shirt and threw it on the stool, covering her shirt.

She moved her hands over his large shoulders, amazed at the strength in his body now. She felt along his biceps and then across to his chest where his defined pectoral muscles flexed beneath her touch. She marveled at the movement under her palms. "You're so big."

His whole torso tensed. "I promise, I won't hurt you."

CHAPTER NINE

You've already done that. Cole jerked at the memory of his dream. He studied Lacey's face, afraid her next words would end it all.

She frowned. "I'm not worried about that. I want to see the new Cole and every inch of muscle you've put on…everywhere."

Her fingers had fluttered down over his abdominals and hooked themselves into the waistband of his jeans. Shit. He was hard as a rock as it was. "Are you sure you want to see everything? I don't want to scare you."

"Cole Hatcher, I'm not some prissy country miss. Now get those clothes off."

He chuckled and stood. He'd forgotten about the bossy side of his woman. Despite her tiny size, she had a backbone of iron. If she wanted a show, a show she'd have…as long as he stayed focused on her face. Looking at her breasts in that see-through mesh would make him lose it, never mind the tiny piece of material covering the place he most wanted to sink his cock into.

He moved their clothing to the top of her dresser and sat on the stool. Then he held his foot straight out so it was positioned between her legs. "A little help?"

She grasped his boot in her hands and pulled as he maneuvered his foot out. "Next."

He lifted the other foot and they removed the boot easily, working together like they used to. Losing no time, he pulled his socks off and draped them over his boots. Lacey's gaze never left him. It made him feel powerful, like he could do anything he wanted and right now he wanted to make love to her, but he wanted her very wet and ready.

Slowly, he stood and unzipped his jeans. Pushing the pants from his legs, he added them to the pile of clothing, turning his back to her in his white underwear.

"Oh my gosh."

He looked at her over his shoulder. "What?"

"Your back is huge." She practically drooled.

He couldn't resist and tensed his back muscles.

She made the tiny squeak she used to make when they made love and he spun around.

"How did it get like that?"

He shrugged. "We have weight equipment at the station so we can stay in shape for our annual physical tests. That and taking care of the horses will do it."

She continued to stare, open-mouthed, so he finished undressing and added his underwear to the pile.

Her gaze riveted to his erection, which had to be harder than a branding iron and almost as hot.

He held his arms out to the sides. "As you wished."

Lacey licked her lips. "You have changed so much. Heck, Cole, you're a stud."

He smiled and strode toward her. He was about to pull her against him when her hands closed around his cock. Her touch sent need straight to his balls and he froze. She moved her hands over every inch of it as if she'd never seen it before. He'd come in seconds if he let her continue that.

Gently, he released his cock from her hands and lifted her farther back on the bed. He settled himself over her, his knees between her legs, leaning on his hands. He finally allowed himself to gaze at her mesh-covered nipples. They were hard and straining against their prison. He lowered his head and licked across each nub.

Lacey's hiss was the only sound in the room. A sound he loved hearing. He teased each nipple in turn, sucking at it through the thin material, the hard nub welcoming his mouth. Then he scraped his teeth across it. Lacey's squeak had him looking up at her face.

"Please, Cole."

He let the hardened nub go, loving that she was in a hurry.

She reached behind her and the bra loosened. "Please take them."

He knelt up and pulled the bra away before cupping both breasts. They filled his hands perfectly. "You're so beautiful."

She gazed at his chest. "So are you." Her hands came up to cover his pectorals and then moved over his stomach.

He'd missed her touch. Delicate fingers explored the contours of his abdominals and he couldn't keep them from tensing, afraid she'd touch his erection, which would end his exploration of her, and he so wanted to explore. When instead her fingertips moved back up, slightly scraping at his skin, his balls tightened as memories of the scratches she'd caused in the past doubled his anticipation.

Pulling his attention back to her nipples, he circled one with his tongue, enjoying the sight of her areola puckering. The aroma of her perfume rose from her chest to mix with the scent of her readiness. That she was slippery between her legs had him stopping to take a deep breath to rope in his own need.

Lacey arched her back, pushing her breast closer, wanting more. He couldn't deny her. He took her hard nub between his teeth and bit lightly. Her hands grasped his head and a tiny moan escaped her throat. The new sound from her made him want more. He sucked her nipple into his mouth, taking her areola with it, and he tongued it inside.

"Oh gosh, Cole." Her voice was barely above a whisper, yet it sent a shiver down his back and into his ass.

He grinned inside, pleased he could bring her pleasure again. It had been too long. Finally, letting her well-attended-to nipple go, he kissed his way down her smooth stomach, and pulled down the tiny piece of material covering her entrance, revealing the small patch of trimmed golden hair that guarded her clit. Her hands dropped to the sides, but her hips rose and he easily slid off her thong.

Spreading her legs wider, he licked across the patch of hair before flicking his tongue over her hard clit, eliciting another moan from her. Giving in to his own need, he lapped down to her opening, moaning at her familiar taste, one that had always made him lose control. But he was a man now, not a boy, and he forced himself to hold back as he pushed her folds aside with his tongue before thrusting it inside.

Lacey's moan filled the room, that new sound he wanted to hear more of. He used his fingers to spread her, giving his tongue better access, and he licked upward to her clit before diving once more into her sweetness. Her sheath contracted around his tongue and he stilled. He was going to come.

He lifted his head away. Kneeling, he spread his knees apart and pulled her ass onto his thighs, her opening just touching his cock. Looking down at where they were about to join, he couldn't quite believe he would fit inside her tiny body. He hesitated.

"Cole?"

"Hmm?" They had done this when they were younger, but would he hurt her now?

"Look at me." Her raspy voice brought his gaze up to meet hers.

The need in her eyes fired his to the brink of his control. His love for this woman was deeper than the Grand Canyon. How could he have ever let her go?

"Now, Cole. I want you inside me now." At her bossy tone, he grasped her hips, ready to plunge inside.

"Shit." He pulled his pelvis back, too tempted to sink into her immediately.

"What?" Lacey's voice was filled with impatience.

"I forgot protection."

She looked up at the ceiling as if she counted to ten. When her gaze returned to his, it softened. "I'm on the Pill and I got tested this month, so I'm okay. How about you?"

He relaxed. Of course she was on the Pill. They'd only used

condoms in high school because they were easy to obtain without their parents knowing. "I was tested last month. You are the first."

"Thank the saints for small favors. Now can you please bury that handsome cock inside me before I explode?"

This time he grinned at her and raised his eyebrow. Something about her anxiousness gave him the tiny bit of control he needed. He corralled her pleasure and he would make sure it met all her expectations. Propping her ass back onto his thighs, he pulled her hips closer. "What's the rush?"

"Cole Hatcher, if you don't—"

He couldn't hold back the hiss as he drove himself home, sinking into her wet heat. Grasping her hips against him, he savored the feel of her sheath clenching him. They fit together as they always had. He was home.

Her hand covered his. "I love the feel of you inside me."

His heart leapt at her first words, but as she continued, he chastised himself. She couldn't trust him with her heart yet, but she would. Now that he had her back in his life, he wouldn't let anyone keep them apart, even her. "You don't feel too bad either." He winked, happy to see her cheeks flush.

Not giving her time to respond, he slowly pulled back his hips, but kept the head of his cock at her entrance. His butt tensed with the need to thrust back in. Instead, he let himself glide inside slowly. When he could go no farther, he let go of her hips and her heels dug into the mattress to keep them joined.

He moved his hands up her waist and took both nipples between his fingers, rolling them gently, his cock jerking as her hips undulated against him. He held her hard nubs as long as he could but the sucking of her sheath combined with the moans she emitted, finally broke his control. He grasped her hips and held them against him. He was meant to be inside her.

Her whimper echoed his own need and he pulled back and thrust forward. The rush of sensation made his balls tighten. Grasping her hips hard, he pulled out and pushed forward again, desperately hoping he could hang on until she hit her orgasm.

Lacey's pants at his thrusts turned to high-pitched moans that sent need coursing straight to his groin. Unable to keep it slow, he pumped into her again. Faster, harder, pulling her to him as he pushed into her.

"Yes. Yes. Yes." Lacey's words egged him on, letting him know she was close.

Just a little longer. He had to hold back—

"Uhh." Lacey's sheath pulsed against him, her release triggering his own as familiar squeals filled the room. He pistoned inside her as he let go, bursts of pleasure flowing through his body and into her, satisfying, completing.

As he slowed his movements, he gazed at the woman he loved. Her face was flush, her body limp, her eyes closed, and she was radiant. Her eyes opened and a slow smile curved her lips. "Finally."

Lacey felt the walls around her heart fall as Cole laughed. He was the missing piece in her life all these years. No matter how much she tried to move on, he'd kidnapped her heart and now he gave it back. Maybe they *could* have a future.

Cole gazed at her, the love in his eyes filling her soul. "I promise, next time I'll be more prompt."

The idea of making love again had her tightening her sheath.

"Whoa there. Give a stallion a chance to recover."

She wrinkled her brow. "Stallion? Really? You don't think much of yourself, do you?"

"Hey." He shrugged. "I don't hear you complaining."

And he wouldn't. Only he could make her feel completely whole. "No, no complaints."

Cole leaned down and kissed her, his lips against hers, gentle and loving. She wrapped her arms around him, wishing they could stay like this forever.

He pulled away and rubbed the side of her hip. "I hope I didn't hold too tight."

Sugar, there was no way he could. "No. I'm glad you held on because I couldn't. In fact, I don't think I could stand right now if you promised me a closet full of lingerie."

"Really?" Cole's prideful smirk had her laughing inside.

"I think I could sleep for a week starting right now."

"Oh no you don't." He scooped his arms under her back and lifted her up, so she sat on his thighs, his cock still inside her, her breasts pressed against his hard chest.

The rush of excitement the position caused had her sheath tightening again. She chuckled at his intake of breath. Served him right. "Hmm, I think I like this new position."

"Racy Lacey, you are going to kill me for sure." He paused. "Unless you happened to have a couple popsicles that might help me recover?"

She laughed. "Are you still eating orange popsicles?"

"Of course. They are one of the five main food groups."

She hugged him tight. "Then we better go into the kitchen."

He pulled back to look at her. "You have orange popsicles?"

"Oh, I'm not sure what flavors I have, but I definitely have popsicles." She smiled widely, ridiculously pleased she could accommodate his request.

His open laugh shook them both and had her stomach doing summersaults. Both her heart and her sheath approved of his laughter.

Cole grasped her tight and moved one of his legs off the bed. "What are you doing?"

He ignored her and stood on that one leg. While holding her tight, he moved his other off so he could stand. "We're getting popsicles."

Her heart raced as he strode toward her kitchen, keeping them together as if he couldn't stand to be parted from her. Darn, the man was strong.

When he reached her small kitchen, he must have realized he couldn't maneuver to open the freezer with her in his arms. She kept her lips closed, curious to see what he would do.

After a couple seconds, he turned around to face her kitchen table. The pale oak furniture was rarely used for eating. Half the time it was where she worked on her computer and the other half of the time it was bare, like now.

Cole plunked her down on the edge and carefully disengaged them. "Cole, what are you doing?"

"Just stay there while I check out what you have to offer." His gaze roved over her body before he finally turned to the fridge.

Oh gosh, her nipples were hard just from that simple look. What was it about this man that turned her on so much? Cole's back muscles rippled as his hand searched her freezer. She held her breath, waiting for him to spot the popsicles.

"Ah, here they are." He bent over, showing her his tight ass and the ball sac that hung below.

Duh. It was pretty obvious why he had her libido revving. The man was built.

He turned around, the popsicle box in his hand, and set it on the table next to her. "Let's see what we have." After rummaging through it, he pulled out a red popsicle and handed it to her. "You can have this one."

She grinned, tickled by his seriousness over the flavors, and quickly unwrapped her designated treat.

"I'll take this one. It's the only orange. You must have eaten the rest." He frowned at her as if she'd committed a sacrilege.

She shrugged, barely holding back a smile, and instead popped the icy tip into her mouth.

Cole's stare riveted to her mouth. She took advantage of his attention and slowly guided the popsicle deeper, as far as it would go before letting it slide out. Then she lapped up the sides, glancing at him to be sure he watched.

He watched, but then growled and his large hand closed over hers. "Stop."

She released the popsicle from her mouth and fluttered her lashes innocently. "Why?"

He grasped her chin with his free hand and kissed her, his tongue mimicking the movement she'd done with the popsicle. His hand moved to the back of her head and he didn't stop until she was breathless. "That's why."

Her heart pounded in her chest as she took in large gulps of air to cool down her hot body. She stuck the popsicle back in her mouth and kept it there, letting it cool her mouth.

Cole must have been as hot as she was because he ripped off the wrapper of his popsicle and proceeded to bite hunks off it. She wanted to laugh at how silly they were, but a quick glance at his cock confirmed silliness was the furthest thing from his mind.

She pulled the pop out of her mouth. "Do you like it?"

He looked at her in puzzlement. "It's a popsicle, what's not to like?"

"Yes, but it's a sugar-free popsicle. With all Selma's cooking, I try to snack light when I'm home."

Cole shook his head. "I don't care what size you are." He bit off the last piece of his popsicle and threw the stick in the trash nearby. Then he foraged in the popsicle box for another.

"You say all the right things, Cole Hatcher." She lay her hand on his chest, unable to resist touching him another minute.

"And so do you." He pulled out another popsicle, a purple one.

She bit off the final piece of her own and let it cool her mouth as she handed the stick to him to throw away. "What did I say?"

He unwrapped the popsicle and looked at her, a devilish grin on his face. "Sugar-free."

"Are you on a diet?"

He opened her legs and positioned himself between them, his hard cock teasing her. "I guess I am. A diet of you. Good to know I won't be eating any calories."

"Cole, I think—"

"Lie back." His command surprised her.

"On the table?"

He nodded. Oh wow, she'd never had sex on a table before. Even as she lay back, her folds moistened.

Cole stared down at her, licking at the popsicle, something he never did. He always bit them. But he made no move to enter her. If he was going to eat that before doing anything, she might fall asleep by time he finished.

"Now put your hands behind your back so you're lying on them."

"Why?" Though she asked, she did as he wished, liking how it tilted her opening to a better angle.

He grinned. "Because I don't want you to stop me." He took the popsicle from his mouth and circled one of her nipples.

"Oh Cole." Her nubs hardened on contact and her sheath contracted.

He leaned over and sucked off the purple liquid. Then he did the same with her other nipple. She couldn't help it. She arched upward, loving the contrast of ice cold and warm mouth.

He ran the popsicle along her lips then licked them clean. Though she opened her mouth, he refused her silent invitation. Instead, he brought the icy dessert to just above her mons.

She swallowed hard. "You can't." Her words were barely a whisper and the complete opposite of her body's wishes.

Once again, he grinned mischievously. "I can." He lay the tip of the popsicle against her clit and she dropped her hips, trying to run from the cold, but Cole only chuckled. "Come on, Lacey. If you brave the cold, I can warm you up."

Her heart beat faster, her throat went dry, and her nipples hardened more even as her sheath loosened, wanting intrusion. She nodded, unable to voice her assent.

Once again, Cole lowered the popsicle head to her clit and she forced herself to remain still, experiencing its chilling sensation on her sensitive nub. Within seconds it was removed and Cole's mouth covered her. He sucked gently then licked all around it. Her body revved at his ministrations, wanting more.

It got more. The popsicle once again lay against her clit, tightening her sheath and bringing every nerve to the breaking point before Cole followed it with his mouth, laving away at the juices. She felt them dripping down to her opening and hoped he followed them there. He didn't disappoint. His tongue licked all around her folds, readying her for his penetration.

Again the popsicle moved to her clit, her body expecting it and welcoming it this time. But then he drew it down her folds toward her opening and she held her breath. He wouldn't.

As her entrance grew cold, Cole's tongue licked at her clit. She moaned at the hot and cold sensation. It was so good. Every part of her was caught up in the maelstrom of sensation, bringing her to the edge of sanity.

Then the popsicle slid inside.

She squealed as her orgasm erupted, ice and fire rampaging through her, making her shiver even as her body heated with exquisite exhilaration. She pulled her hands out from beneath her and grabbed the table as the powerful pleasure hit her.

"Aw shit." Cole's voice penetrated her euphoria a moment before the cold popsicle disappeared and he replaced it with his warm, hard cock that forced her sheath to widen.

Her slowing orgasm sped back up as Cole thrust into her, rocking her body on the table, pushing into her until her world exploded again. "Cole!" She yelled his name and he pulled her up to hold against him as he finished his own release.

She grasped on to him, her body shuddering. He was her rock in a microburst of orgasm.

As his thrusts slowed to a stop, he wrapped his other arm around her and held her close. The pounding of his heart against her ear made her feel safe.

"Shit, Lacey, that was…"

She nodded against his chest. There were no words to describe what it was like to have so much pleasure with the person she loved. She wanted to tell him, but her throat closed, her stupid mind still refusing to yield up everything.

Cole leaned back and tipped her chin up. "I don't know about you, but I'm wiped."

She smiled sleepily. "Me too."

He nodded. "Can you wrap your ankles around my waist?"

She did as he asked, switching her arms to link her hands around his neck. Then he strode back to the bedroom as if she weighed nothing. There were definite advantages to having a strong cowboy firefighter for a lover.

Cole sat on the bed. She unhooked her ankles and pulled herself off him, but her knees weren't ready for her weight, and she stumbled.

He scooped her up and lay her down on the bed. Climbing in beside her, he pulled the light blanket over them.

She rested her head on his massive shoulder. Muscles were so much nicer than a pillow. Then she placed her palm on his chest, exhausted but content.

Cole kissed the top of her head. "I've missed you."

She wanted to respond, even parted her lips, but sleep won and she happily drifted away.

~~~~~

The ear-splitting scream woke Cole faster than the fire alarm at the station, but it took a minute to figure out where he was. The thrashing in the bed finally penetrated and he pulled Lacey against him. "Lacey, wake up."

Fear coursed through him at her screaming. "Lacey! Wake up!" He shook her and her eyes opened wide.

"Cole." She grasped him about the neck and sobbed.

Holy shit. Her body shook within his arms and he felt her heart pounding. It had to be one hell of a nightmare. Fuck, his own adrenaline still coursed through him just from the terror in her scream.

Stroking her back with one hand, he held her tightly against him. "It's okay. Everything's all right. It was just a nightmare." To call what she'd experienced a bad dream would be an insult. He'd only heard that kind of fear in a woman's voice once before when a mother's baby was trapped inside her burning home and one of his men held her back as Cole raced inside. Luckily, he'd been able to save the child before the ceiling collapsed.

"Shhh, it's okay now. You're safe."

Her head came off his shoulder. "But you weren't."

He looked into her watery eyes filled with grief and his heart constricted. She dreamed of him? "Why wasn't I?" He stroked her tangled tresses away from her face.

"You were trapped in a burning building and it collapsed on top of you."

A shiver ran up his spine. He had to admit he bought into many of the superstitions his fellow firefighters had. A dream with a trapped firefighter was never a good thing. Then again, it wasn't his dream.

Her hand came up and pulled his head toward her lips. Complying with her silent request, he kissed her. But it wasn't his mouth she wanted. She kissed his lips, the stubble on his chin, his cheek and finally his nose.

He pulled away and looked at her. She feared his death. It meant her heart felt so much more than she admitted. A surge of relief washed through him. There was hope for them. "But I'm okay. In fact I rarely go into the buildings anymore and if I make captain, it will happen even less often." He grinned. "I hope I was doing something heroic like saving someone."

Her face froze.

"Lacey, what is it?" He stroked her back again, hoping to see color return to her face.

"You were. You were looking for me in the carriage house, but I was outside. I've been having these nightmares every night since the fire here."

His mind raced at her admission. Were her nightmares a reflection of her involvement? He stared into her concerned face. Maybe the Orson fire *had* been an accident. Maybe she'd forgotten to blow out one of the candles she was so fond of using back then. He glanced around the bedroom. There wasn't a single candle in it. "It could be your subconscious acting out your guilt from long ago. Hopefully, once Sean proves who started this fire, your dreams will go away."

Her eyes turned hard. "Guilt? Guilt for what? I have nothing to feel guilty about."

"That's what I'm saying. They ruled the Orson fire an accident, but you feel guilty about it. Did they ever say what it was? Was it a candle you left burning?"

Her mouth opened then closed. In the next instant she pulled out of his arms, scrambled out of bed and stood. "Get out."

"What? Lacey, what's wrong?" He sat up. What just happened here?

She pointed her finger toward the bedroom door. "I'll tell you what's wrong. You make love to me like I'm the most important woman on earth and yet you still think I started the Orson fire?"

"I made love to you because I love you. What has that got to do with the past?"

She swallowed hard, but her scowl tightened. "You said you believed me. How can you love me and still think I started that fire? That's why you dumped me in the first place! I don't want a man in my life who can't believe in me no matter what. Now get out."

Fuck. He rose from the bed and towered over her. "So you're saying you had nothing at all to do with your parents' carriage house burning to the ground."

She shook her head. "Just go."

He wanted her back in his arms in the worst way. Part of him told him to lie, tell her he believed her, but as much as he wanted to, he couldn't do it. Grabbing up his clothes, he strode into the living room. "If you want me out of your bed right now, fine. But I'm not leaving this house. There are some crazy-ass college students out there, and I'm not about to let them anywhere near you."

Something akin to a growl issued from her tiny body and then the bedroom door slammed shut, a small click making it clear it was locked.

Shit, what the hell?

He put his clothes back on except for his jacket and boots

and eyed the love seat with the cactus-flower patterned pillows. The clock said 3:52 a.m. Two more hours before sunrise and three before he had to leave for a twenty-four-hour shift.

He looked at Lacey's door. Maybe in the morning she'd be more open to a discussion. He didn't want to leave without them talking. She needed to know the fire in Orson didn't matter anymore. He could see now, without his parents pressuring him, that there was no way she could have purposefully started that fire. It was his parents who made him dump Lacey in the first place. A hot mix of hurt from having to break off their relationship in the past and Lacey's rejection of him now burned through his gut like a wildfire.

He wouldn't lose her again, no matter what. They *had* to come to an understanding that would mean they stayed in each other's lives. He would accept nothing less.

Glancing once more at the love seat, he swept up the pillows, pushed the coffee table aside and lay on the area rug. He probably wouldn't sleep much, which was just as well. As soon as he heard Lacey come out, they would talk.

CHAPTER TEN

Lacey tiptoed to her bedroom door and listened. Maybe Cole had left. She certainly hoped so. She'd been stupid to think he'd changed his mind about her guilt. Tears welled in her eyes as pain ripped through her wounded heart, but she brushed them away. She needed to focus on Cole and what an ass he was.

Quietly, she turned the knob and peeked out. Her breath caught at the sight of him stretched out across her living room in blue jeans and dress shirt. He lay on his back, one hand resting on his stomach, the other thrown to the side, his face toward her. In his sleep, he appeared so approachable, reasonable and too darn handsome.

She forced herself to look away and instead concentrated on slipping out of her room and toward the front door. She shook her head as the knob turned. They'd never even locked it last night. Not smart, but it made it easier to leave. Silently, she closed the door behind her and took a deep breath. Yeah, she was a chicken not to wake him, but her throat was too raw from crying and she promised herself she would focus on how mad she was at him, not on how he'd hurt her…again.

She usually walked home, but because Cole was with her last night, she'd taken a golf cart, which would make her escape that much faster. Thankful the carts were so quiet, she stepped on the pedal and drove to the main building. It was only a bit past four thirty, but hopefully no one would be awake to notice when she arrived.

That hope died as she pulled around front and found Hunter standing outside the lobby doors. Great, just what she needed, another cowboy to interfere in her life. After exiting her cart, she walked toward him, but couldn't quite muster a smile. "Good morning, Hunter."

He pointedly scanned the eastern horizon before looking back at her and tipping his hat. "Not morning yet."

She laughed nervously. "I guess not, but I have some billing I need to catch up on."

He studied her. His gaze detached as if he were cataloging supplies instead of looking at a human being. She really needed to read his file. With that in mind, she reached for the door.

"You couldn't sleep."

She froze in mid-motion. "Why do you say that?"

"You have nightmares and they wake you up, but even once awake you can't shake the feelings they cause."

She stared at him in shock. He no longer looked at her, his eyes scanning the resort instead.

She gave an uncomfortable chuckle. "I better get to work." She grasped the door handle, anxious to go inside.

"Might want to stop in the kitchen for some ice. It will help the swelling go down before anyone else comes in." His gaze returned to her, his eyes hard. "Do you want me to take him down for you?"

"No! I mean, no. I mean I…" She chickened out for the second time in less than thirty minutes and simply walked into the lobby, too shaken to answer him.

Once in the backroom, she checked her face in the mirror. Sugar, her eyes were even more puffy than back at her place. She looked like she had two black eyes, only without the black. No wonder Hunter told her about the ice and offered to go after Cole. That was a fight she hoped never happened. Cole had a lot more muscle, at least it appeared that way, but Hunter was like a cross bow, pulled tight and held back by the smallest of mechanisms.

Torn between her curiosity about their new security guard and a need to make her face presentable, she chose the latter and headed for the kitchen. Grabbing a couple ice cubes and a towel, she placed it over her puffy eyes.

She didn't understand it. How could Cole believe her about the Poker Flat fire yet not in regards to her parents' carriage house? And then to make love to her still believing her guilty? It didn't make any sense. More importantly, knowing he still felt that way, what was she to do? She felt as if her heart held on to a tiny mesquite branch while the flood of a monsoon pulled at it, threatening to rip it away. She had to find dry ground somewhere.

Her stomach growled, reminding her she was technically on dry ground at the moment and it needed sustenance. She lowered the ice, but didn't move to find something to eat. She had quite a workout last night. He'd been so focused on her, making her feel sensations she hadn't felt before, even when they were together in the past. They'd been so young back then and very inexperienced. Was she expecting too much from him?

The batwing doors to the kitchen swung open and Adriana sauntered in. Her hair, usually beautifully straight, was a mess and her blouse was held closed by only two buttons. "Honey, what are you doing here this late?"

"Late? It's almost morning."

Adriana brushed by her and opened the refrigerator. "Crap, I lost track of time."

Lacey studied her coworker. Her skirt was on backward. "Was he good?"

"You mean were *they* good?" The woman turned around, the leftover Sopapilla Cheesecake in her hands.

"More than one?" Her face heated at the idea.

The smile that curved Adriana's lips was sultry with a capital S. "Three. It was supposed to be four, but the fourth found action elsewhere."

Lacey swallowed as she envisioned three Coles making love to her. There was no way the men Adriana had sex with could have been as good as Cole last night or the woman wouldn't be able to walk.

"Do you want some?" Adriana had cut herself a large piece of the cheesy cinnamon dessert.

Lacey had planned on her usual bagel, but after the night she'd had, she deserved a little extra sugar. "Sure."

The woman's head snapped up. "Really?" She studied her then looked at the towel with ice on the counter. "What happened? And don't tell me 'nothing.'"

She squirmed. The problem with a small staff was they all

knew one another's business. "Why don't you ask Hunter? He seems to have figured everything out."

"Hunter? I haven't seen him since the morning the deputy sheriff was here. I mean the *last* morning the deputy sheriff was here, yesterday I think it was. Besides, why would I ask him? I don't know him, but I know you."

She looked away, not sure where to start.

"Do you want me to shoot him for you?" Adriana's free hand found her hip, a sure sign she was dead serious.

"No. Please don't."

"But he hurt you again."

Lacey shrugged. "Yes and no. It's the same old hurt. I thought he'd changed his mind, but I was wrong. Instead he rubbed salt in the wound."

"You slept with him."

She nodded, blinking back a new round of tears. She clasped her hands in front of her. She was so stupid.

"Was he good?"

She snapped her gaze to Adriana's face in surprise. "What?"

The woman wiggled her brows. "Was he good in bed?"

Heat built in her cheeks as she looked away. He'd been amazing. His hands, his lips, his tongue, his….

"Ah, he was." Adriana leaned her elbows on the counter and rested her chin on her hands. "He made you hot and ready and brought you to the best orgasm you've ever had, right?"

Lacey sighed. "Yes."

"He's a big man and you're so small." Adriana smiled knowingly. "That's one perfect combination."

Lacey felt heat rise in her cheeks. "Weren't you getting breakfast or something?"

The bartender laughed and straightened. "Yes, I was and here's yours." She handed over a plate with a large piece of cheesecake on it. "Honey, just remember sex and love are two different things. Sex I know," she winked, "very well, but I haven't a clue what love feels like, so if you need advice about sex, I'm your go-to person. But if your heart is involved, you better find someone else to talk to."

She wasn't sure there was anyone who could really help with the mess she'd made of her heart.

Adriana picked up her plate and sauntered toward the exit. She stopped and looked over her shoulder. "By the way, if you dump your firefighter, I know a couple deputy sheriffs who would love to meet you."

Lacey scowled and the woman let out another laugh before pushing through the batwing doors.

Picking up her cheesecake, she headed to her office to start the coffee. There was a good chance Cole Hatcher would stop by on his way out this morning and she had to decide what she would say to him besides goodbye.

As the clock on her desk ticked and the time for Cole to be at work had passed, she felt a strange mix of relief and disappointment. Relief because she still didn't know what to do about him and disappointment for the same reason.

The thought of Cole gone from her life forever made her heart hitch, a sure sign she loved him. But that was a given. The question was, could she forgive him for not believing her? He believed her about the most recent fire. Was that enough? The adult in her said she'd be a fool not to forgive him, but the child in her stamped her feet and demanded Cole believe her out of love. She was probably being too idealistic.

The door to the resort opened and hope surged through her chest, but the clothed man who walked across the lobby wasn't Cole. It was John.

She forced herself to smile and approached the counter. "Good morning. What a pleasant surprise. Are you coming to spend the day nude?" She doubted he was since he had his bike gear on, but she was hoping he'd come for any reason but her.

"No. Thanks anyway. I prefer to be naked in private or with a special someone." He wiggled his eyebrows at her.

Uh, that wasn't going to happen. If she'd had any thoughts about dating John, her heart nixed them. He was not an option.

"I came to see if you'd like to go for a ride. I always ride on Sundays. Then I thought we could go to that pizza place I talked about. What do you think?"

"What a lovely invitation. Unfortunately, I'm working today."

His disappoint was obvious as his smile disappeared. "Do you ever get a day off?"

She shook her head. "Not really." Of course she'd never asked for one since she had no life. "The resort is so new, Kendra really needs me until it's stable enough to hire more employees. You know how that is. You did say Price Construction was hanging on by a thread as well, right? So you must understand."

John's emotions played across his face. Anger, frustration and finally acceptance that he was beat. "Yeah, I do. We all have to make a living, right?" His smile was wan.

She nodded. "At least until I have a husband who will let me stay home while he works. Until then, I'm kind of stuck."

John literally stepped back and she had to swallow her laugh.

"Right, well, I better get going. Meeting some of my buddies out at Lake Pleasant before we head north."

"Of course. Have a great ride."

He backed away. "I plan on it." Then he swiftly turned and strode out of the lobby.

She chuckled at how quickly marriage could scare most men away. Would Cole feel the same way? She sobered and her belly flipped. Memories of writing Mrs. Lacey Hatcher in her notebooks at school flooded her. She'd always dreamed about them getting married.

How did she feel about it now?

~~~~~

After three hours of driving, Cole exited his truck and stretched his legs. He missed Lacey, but coming to Orson was the right thing to do.

When he'd woken on the floor of Lacey's casita, he'd been shocked to find her gone. That and the fact he was in serious danger of being late for his shift. After catching a ride with Wade to the garage and speaking to him about keeping Lacey safe, he'd barely made it to work. They had one kitchen fire and two ambulance calls, but other than that he'd had all day to think.

By time he'd made it back to Last Chance Ranch, Angel required his undivided attention. He even slept in the barn, not an unknown occurrence for him, which is why he had a cot set up out there. Luckily, her fever broke in the early morning hours.

After calling the vet and getting his visit confirmed, Cole left for Orson. It was time to learn the facts. Lacey insisted she was innocent. The town thought she'd set the fire and his parents said the Town Manager had the charges dropped, but he'd never talked to the fire department directly.

He had a very specific reason for going in person. Sean had called and said all the frat boys they'd caught denied building any campfires even though they copped to the theft charge. Since there was more than one campfire, the chances it was Price Construction making it look like it was someone else was very slim. That left Lacey as a prime suspect.

Striding into the firehouse, he followed the directions to the chief's office upstairs. He knocked on the door and entered when told to.

Cole slowed as he approached the desk. The man who rose from the chair didn't have enough stripes for a chief.

"Hi, I'm Lieutenant Hatcher."

"The chief is off today, I'm Deputy Chief Reynolds. I can see you're far from your station district. Please, have a seat. How can I help you?"

He glanced down at his firehouse t-shirt, glad he'd worn it. It just might help him obtain the information he needed. "Yes, I have family in town, but thought I'd stop by and see if I could get a little information to help the detective working on a case in my district."

The deputy chief leaned back in his chair. "He could have called. I would have been happy to tell him what we know, or sent him the file if it's recent information. We just started computerizing our cases a couple years ago. Getting the older ones into the system isn't a big priority."

Cole was ready for that. "I wasn't sure if my memory was even worth him making the call. I worked a fire about a week ago and there was a woman there who I remembered being accused of setting a fire here about eight years ago. I thought I'd see if my memory was correct before sending Detective Anderson in the wrong direction."

The deputy stroked his mustache. "That was a while back. Which fire was it?"

"It was the old carriage house at the Winters' place."

"Oh I remember that one. I worked it." The deputy nodded. "Yes, wasn't the daughter accused of setting the fire?"

Cole studied the deputy, trying to place him at the fire, but that evening he'd been too focused on Lacey to notice much else. When he'd arrived, she and her dad had been wrapped in blankets by the emergency crew. He was told they both suffered from smoke inhalation after trying to put the fire out. "That's what I remembered, but for some reason the charges were dropped." It would be like Lacey to try to fight a fire she accidently set. It *had* to be an accident.

The deputy walked to a door to his left and opened it. A small room filled with a dozen or so file cabinets was visible. "Do you remember when that fire was?"

The day before he broke it off with the woman he loved? He'd never forget it, April 29th. "I know it was in April. It was after Easter but before prom."

The deputy raised a brow. "Interesting what's important when we're young, huh?"

Cole nodded.

"That narrows it down though."

Cole heard the drawer of a cabinet open and then the man came out, a file in his hand. It took all of Cole's willpower not to jump up and snatch it from him. Instead, he leaned forward, his elbows on his knees, and forced himself to remain seated.

The deputy sat behind the desk and opened the file. "Hmmm, oh yes, I remember, we let the building burn to the ground. Had a couple explosions and the captain didn't want to risk anyone. Luckily, the girl got out before we arrived."

Cole's heart froze. *Lacey was inside?* "Do you mean the woman accused of the fire was in the building when it started?"

The deputy nodded absently as he perused the paperwork. "It says here that the father and daughter were treated for smoke inhalation. Apparently, he saw the flames and knew she was inside. He couldn't get to her, but told her to wrap herself in a blanket and brave the doorway. That's not an easy feat for a civilian. The father was trying to soak the door from the outside with his garden hose and the smoke got to him."

His chest tightened. He'd almost lost her that night and didn't even know it. Why didn't she say anything? The answer came as quickly as the question. He never let her. He just broke her heart, never even asking her if she started the fire. He was such an idiot. "If she was inside then why was she charged with arson?"

"Good question." The deputy chief turned a couple pages in the file. "It looks like those charges were originally based upon a witness. The neighbor had been driving into town and said she saw the girl spreading gasoline around the outside of the building." The deputy looked up and shook his head. "Charges wouldn't be made based solely on a witness today. If I remember correctly, the nearest neighbor was at least a mile away. She would have had to be driving pretty slow to see a gasoline can specifically."

Cole nodded agreement, but clasped his hands tight to keep from leaning across the desk and taking the file out of the deputy's hands. "So if those charges were dropped, did they ever determine what caused the fire?"

"Yes, I saw it here a minute ago." The deputy shuffled the paperwork around. "Ah here it is. It was ruled accidental. They determined the fire started from hot charcoal thrown on the ground too close to the building. Probably a group of teenagers having a little barbecue. Didn't even realize what they'd done. That girl was lucky to get out alive."

Cole felt the blood drain from his face and his stomach rumbled. He'd almost killed Lacey. *He* started the fire.

"Hey, Lieutenant, you okay?"

Cole forced the single word past his constricted throat. "Bathroom?"

The deputy pointed. "Right across the hall."

Cole spun out of the chair and ran for the bathroom. Slamming the door behind him, he knelt at the toilet. His stomach roiled and bile crept up his throat. He took deep breaths, trying to relax his insides while his mind took off like a wild mustang. All these years he'd thought Lacey started the fire and it was him. *Him.*

Stupid teenager. One-track mind. He'd cooked her dinner on the hibachi, wanting to please her. She said she'd clean up while he took care of the coals and whoever finished first had to undress the other.

He ran outside and instead of digging a hole far away from the building, he threw the coals on the ground outside near the door, planning to cover them later. But by time he left, he'd forgotten all about them.

And she'd stayed.

His stomach stopped twisting and he stood. She could have

died and it would have been all his fault. Shit, she'd been right to keep him at arm's length. Some firefighter he was.

After splashing cold water on his face, he wiped it with a paper towel and looked at who he was today, seeing vestiges of that young, dumb kid he used to be. He didn't deserve Lacey, but he still couldn't imagine a life without her in it. Even if he had to spend that life making it up to her, he had to have her back. She was innocent. He was the guilty party.

Taking one more deep breath, he walked into the deputy's office.

"You okay?"

Cole nodded. "Yeah, I don't think the lunch I had at the truck stop on my way down here agreed with me."

"I hear you." The deputy grimaced. "I read the rest of this file and you won't believe what prompted the arson charge. This little town was a regular Payton Place back then."

"It isn't anymore?"

"Good point." The deputy grinned. "But listen to this. The neighbor's daughter had a crush on the girl's boyfriend, so the neighbor thought if she could break them up, her daughter could go to the prom with the boy. What some people won't do."

While the deputy shook his head, Cole tried to remember who the neighbor was. Hopefully, the name Hatcher was nowhere in the record. Actually, he'd bet his parents made sure that was how it was.

"So it looks like this girl being at your fire is no more than a coincidence."

Cole nodded. "I guess so, but I had to check it out. It's rare for the same person to be at two suspicious fires."

The deputy snapped the file shut, and held it out. "If you want, you're welcome to make copies of this. We have a machine down the hall."

He stared at the damning file. His aversion to it was now as strong as his need to have it was just minutes earlier. "No, I'm good. Like you said, there's no connection." He stood, anxious to return to Poker Flat and Lacey. "Thank you for taking the time."

The deputy stood as well. "No problem. It was a nice walk down memory lane. Now," he pointed to a pile of paperwork on the right side of the desk, "it's back to reality."

Cole held out his hand. "I guess that's what I have to look forward to if I get promoted too many times."

The deputy grasped his hand and shook. "Captain is good. No politics until you move higher."

"I'll remember that." Cole nodded and let himself out. He waved to the guys in the garage and strode to his truck. Turning the engine over, he set the air conditioner on full blast and leaned back.

Shit. He'd come to Orson to learn the truth, but the truth had changed his life on so many levels. It showed him what a stupid kid he'd been and how much time he'd wasted without Lacey in his life. But it also shone a light on his parents and their selfishness. If only he'd been a little smarter, a little more observant…like Lacey.

There was nothing he could do about the past, but there was a hell of a lot he could do about the future. Cole leaned forward and put the truck into gear. A three-hour drive back to Phoenix and another twenty-four-hour shift meant he had a long time to plan. One way or another, he would convince Lacey she was this cowboy's match.

~~~~~

Cole parked his truck in the garage and looked for Billy. It was early yet, but still the older man should have been ready for guests.

Striding past the barrier, his boots kicked up dry Arizona dust. The firefighter in him grimaced at the fire potential, but the cowboy in him just wanted to see Lacey.

He walked to the ridge and scanned the resort. Billy was nowhere in sight. One golf cart pulled away from the main building and headed for the stables. It was probably Wade. Cole waved his arms, but the cart continued across the fork and behind the barn.

He had two choices, piss off Kendra and drive his large pick up down over the bridge or call the front desk and risk Lacey hanging up on him. Then again he did have Wade's cellphone number, but that would appear desperate. He wasn't there…yet.

Taking a deep breath, he called the front desk.

"Good morning, Poker Flat Nudist Resort, Lacey speaking."

"Lacey, it's Cole." The silence on the other end didn't bode well.

"What do you want? I thought you'd left." The coldness in her voice didn't bode well either.

He squinted at the horizon. "I did. I had to work, but I'm back and I need to talk to you."

"We don't have anything to talk about." His stomach fell to his toes. Shit. This wasn't going to be easy. But his grandfather always said, "The best things in life are the ones you work hardest for."

"I think we do. Could you send Billy up to the garage with a golf cart?"

"Billy's not there?"

"No, he's not."

The silence on the other end lasted too long. "Lacey? You still there?"

"Yes. I was looking out the lobby window at his casita to see if his cart was there but it isn't." Her worry for the older man was clear in her voice. "If Billy doesn't show up for work, Kendra will fire him. That was one of his stipulations of employment."

That was a little harsher than the typical employment policies, but he was also aware the staff Kendra had gathered together wasn't exactly the typical. "If you can send someone up for me, I could go look for him and no one would be the wiser."

"Okay." The call ended on her end.

He watched the main building nervously, hoping Lacey wasn't just getting him off the phone so she could look for Billy. After a couple minutes, Lacey herself came out.

Shit. She *had* said that to get him off the phone. It looked like he'd have to call Wade after all. His phone rang, but he didn't recognize the number. It could be another horse call. "Hello?"

"Cole?" Lacey's voice sounded anxious.

"Yeah, it's me."

"I'm on my way. Could you check around the outside of the garage and see if Billy's cart is parked there. He could be sleeping out of sight."

"Will do."

She ended the call again, but now he had her number. "Thank you, Lacey."

He strode back toward the garage, heading east of it to check out the back side, but nothing was there, only what was left of the dead campfire he'd told Sean about on the north end. Walking all the way around, he checked the south side, but he was pretty sure he would have noticed a cart on his way in. Nothing.

As he came around the front, Lacey pulled up. She was dressed in a pretty lavender dress with short sleeves and lace all around the hem that hung to her knees. Her white cowboy boots and hat made her pretty enough to eat.

She jumped from her golf cart. "Anything?"

He shook his head. It was all he could do not to grab her up and hug her tight. But she was all business.

"Help me check between the cars. He may have fallen asleep sitting against one."

He tipped his hat. "You mean he may have passed out?"

She frowned. "Yes, that's what I mean."

He took one end of the garage and she took the other and they met in the middle. Still no Billy. "Does he do this often?"

She clasped her hands in front of her. "No. He's never done it before. That's partly why I'm so worried."

He put his hands on her shoulders, ignoring how stiff she became. "Listen, we'll find him. Let's check the barn next. He's been known to pass out in there on occasion."

A glimmer of hope shone in her eyes. "How do you know that?"

"Wade gave Billy his own stall so he wouldn't piss off Kendra by being visible to guests."

"I hope he's there."

He placed one hand over both of hers. "Come, I'll drive."

She nodded, but as he moved forward she pulled her hands away. He sighed inwardly, but wouldn't give up.

At the barn, he and Lacey checked all the empty stalls. No Billy. Now even he was growing concerned. Wade's cart was at his office building. Maybe they should ask him if he'd seen Billy, but then he'd be obligated to tell Kendra. They returned to the cart. "Where to next?"

"I don't know." Lacey's voice had risen with hopelessness. "What if he's hurt? What if he got bit by a rattlesnake or tarantula or scorpion?"

To do that, Billy would have to be in the desert. "What about the horse trails? Are there any wide enough for a golf cart?"

Her eyes brightened. "Yes. The main trail is wide enough for a quarter mile and then only one trail that branches off is wide for another quarter mile."

"Which way?"

Lacey pointed, and Cole drove. By the split in the trail he could sense her losing hope again.

He placed his hand over her clasped ones. "He has to be somewhere here on the resort. Don't worry, we'll find him." She didn't respond, but she didn't pull her hands away either.

The horse trail was meant for horses, so he was forced to use both hands to maneuver the golf cart around cacti and boulders. They had gone a quarter mile when he negotiated the cart around a protruding rock and another golf cart came into view.

"Oh, he has to be around here somewhere." Before he could stop, Lacey jumped from the vehicle and disappeared around a mound of desert rock. "Billy! Oh no, Cole he's here."

He exited the cart and strode past the rocks and around a mesquite tree to where Lacey stood. On the ground lay Billy, an empty bottle of tequila still in his outstretched hand and a smoldering campfire not a foot away.

CHAPTER ELEVEN

Anger surged through Cole like a dust storm. Shit! It was Billy who started the fire. That the man was so irresponsible as to risk the lives of horses, people and the entire desert ecosystem had Cole fisting his hands to stop from throttling the old drunk.

Lacey crouched next to Billy. "Cole, can you help me get him into the golf cart? I need to sober him up before Kendra finds out."

The last thing he wanted to do was save this man's job, but it would be a moot point once Sean learned of this and Cole would make sure he knew. "Lacey, Billy's the one who caused the fire at the new construction site."

"What?" She stood and faced him, an angry blush in her cheeks. "How can you say that?"

"I can't tell you right now because I made a promise to Sean, but I will tell you soon. I need you to bring Billy back to the staff room and keep him there."

"Are you sure?" Her eyes narrowed. "You thought I started the Orson fire and you were wrong, what makes you think you're right about this one?"

"Because I am." He tamped down his frustration. He wasn't about to have an important conversation with her with a drunk lying between them. "Listen, I'll explain everything, even Orson, but right now we need to get him out of the desert before he dehydrates and I need to minimize the wildfire danger."

She looked ready to argue, but finally appeared to accept that now *he* meant business. "Fine."

Having her agreement, he stooped, picked up Billy and propped him in the cart. Except for a short moan, the man didn't wake. "Will you be able to get him to the lobby by yourself?"

"Of course. Aren't you coming?"

"No, I have to call Sean. Have someone go up to the garage to meet him."

Lacey hesitated. "Are you absolutely sure it was Billy?" Her tone had softened.

He hated to disappoint her, but Billy had to be stopped. If they hadn't found him, there very well could have been a wildfire and who knew what devastation it could have done, how many homes lost, how many horses burned, or how many good firefighters hurt. "Yes, I'm afraid I am. Now go."

Lacey's shoulders slumped before she turned the golf cart around and headed back the way they'd come.

He kicked away any possible fire potential and cleared the area from around the smoldering fire. Then he took out his phone.

No cell service. Shit, he should have known. They were deep in the ravine. He hated to disturb evidence, but seeing no alternative, he covered the campfire coals with dirt before heading straight up the side of the canyon. He stopped every few yards and checked again. Finally, he caught a signal and dialed.

"Sean, I know who started the fire at Poker Flat and I have him in custody."

~~~~~

Lacey forced a smile as she explained what paperwork she needed filled out to the newly hired second security guard. The woman was as reserved as Hunter. They should work well together.

Kendra popped her head around the doorframe. "Lacey, I want to see you in my office."

She nodded and quickly set all the paperwork down. "If you have any questions, I'll be back to check on you." She didn't wait for an answer as Kendra's tone was more stern than usual.

Quickly following her boss, she walked toward the chair in front of Kendra's desk.

"Close the door."

Lacey's heart sank. This couldn't be good. When she turned back, Kendra still stood behind her desk.

"Take a seat."

She did as instructed and clasped her hands in front of her tightly to keep from fidgeting.

"While you were helping Selma with the lunch service, I took a call at the front desk that disturbed me. It was from Saguaro Rehabilitation Center."

Oh no. Her stomach somersaulted at the implication. She hadn't wanted her boss to know yet.

Kendra leaned on one hip. "You were going to pay for Billy to dry out. You do know an alcoholic has to want to give up the booze, right?"

She nodded. She was pretty sure she could convince him if she dangled the carrot of coming back to work.

"You also know even if Billy successfully completes the process, I won't hire him back."

"But he could—"

"No. There are no exceptions to the rules. I give people a second chance by inviting them to work here. If they mess up while here, that's it. I don't give third chances. The odds are, there will be a fourth and a fifth and a sixth. If people don't learn from their mistakes the first time, then they won't down the road. As much as I love Billy, I can't risk the rest of my staff and guests."

Lacey sighed. Kendra was right. "What will happen to Billy?"

Her boss pulled out her chair and sat. "I'm going to pay for his rehabilitation. He's not your responsibility. I'm the one who brought him up here from Key West. He was somewhat happy being drunk and homeless down there, but I had to offer him a second chance. After the program, if he makes it through, I'll send him wherever he wants to go. If it's back to the Keys, then fine. If it's somewhere here in Arizona, that's fine too, but I will not hire him back here."

Her heart ached for Billy, but she understood. Kendra had been nothing but kind to all of them, but she had to draw the line somewhere. "Thank you for taking care of him. I couldn't stand the thought of him drunk and homeless on the streets of Phoenix."

Kendra nodded. "I hate to think of him that way too. I should have thought of the rehabilitation first." She looked at Lacey shrewdly. "Then again, he may not go. I'm going to leave it up to you to convince him."

"I will." She wasn't sure how now that Poker Flat was off the table, but she would figure it out. She stood. "Was there anything else?"

"Yes, there is." Kendra's poker face returned, which was never a good sign. It was impossible to tell what she was feeling when she hid behind it.

Lacey sat back down.

"While I was at the front desk I also took a call from Cole Hatcher."

Heat rose in her cheeks. After Sean had taken Billy in for questioning, she'd been so upset, she'd told Cole to leave her alone. He'd reluctantly left, threatening to return, but that was Thursday. He hadn't returned or called on Friday and by this morning she'd given up that he would. If they lost their second chance, it could be laid at her feet. She'd been so upset by Billy's arrest, she couldn't think straight and she'd taken it out on Cole.

"Do you want to know what he said?"

Her heart leaped at getting a message from him. She couldn't resist and nodded.

"He asked to speak to Adriana."

"What? Why? Are you sure?" Lacey jumped from her seat, unable to remain in her chair at Cole's betrayal.

"Yes, I'm sure. I don't know why. I just forwarded his call to the bar."

Why would Cole want to speak to Adriana? Duh, because she's hot, why else? "I better get back to work."

Kendra looked at her with that enigmatic face that revealed nothing and finally nodded. "Go."

Lacey stomped out of her boss's office. It took all her willpower not to slam the door back against the wall. She didn't even look in to see if the new hire needed any help. Instead, she marched across the lobby, through the main gathering room, past the indoor bar and outside where Adriana was restocking for happy hour.

"Why did Cole call you?"

The bartender turned around and raised an eyebrow. "Good afternoon to you too, Lacey."

She kept her fisted hands at her sides. She'd never felt like strangling someone so much as she did her coworker right now. "I'm not in the mood to be polite. Why did Cole call you?"

Adriana laughed. "Honey, he wanted advice."

"About what?"

"Why don't you ask him?" She turned, continuing to add beer to a cooler as if nothing were wrong.

"Because I'm asking you and he's not here."

"Yes, I am."

Lacey whirled at the sound of Cole's voice. At the sight of him, she pressed her hand to her chest as if she could slow the pounding of her heart. He stood there stark naked except for his boots. Her body reacted immediately to all that muscle, warming her from the inside out.

He gazed at her warmly, his green eyes filled with humor. "I was kind of hoping you would be as happy to see me as I am to see you."

Her gaze immediately riveted to his hard cock, sticking straight out as if tempting her to touch it. A whistle from Adriana reminded Lacey of where they were and she stepped in front of him to shield him from the guests at to pool. "What are you doing?"

"I'm enjoying the facilities. I tried to check in at the desk, but no one was there."

She stared up into his eyes. "You're a nudist?"

He grinned as he shook his head. "No, but I was willing to try anything to get you to talk to me." His smile disappeared. "And we *need* to talk, Lacey."

Joy and excitement competed with anger and distrust as she contemplated what she should do.

"Honey, if you two want to talk, you better do it somewhere else because there are three ladies making a beeline over here." Adriana, pointed toward the pool with the beer bottle in her hand.

Lacey looked over her shoulder to see Ginger and a couple much younger women heading straight for the bar. As much as she liked the older woman, she wasn't ready for a decision made by committee. "Come on."

She grabbed Cole's hand and headed for the staff room. It wasn't until they were in the lobby that she remembered the new employee. She didn't want her to see Cole. With no options left, she pulled him outside and around the corner to a semiprivate and shady side of the building.

She let go of his hand. "So—"

In one swift movement, Cole wrapped his arms around her and kissed her. As his tongue swept into her mouth, her body tingled. Her arms were trapped by her sides, but she still leaned into his kiss, his hard cock pressing into her stomach.

When he finally released her, she stumbled and he grasped her shoulders to steady her. "I wanted to do that since the last time I saw you."

How was a girl supposed to think when he pulled a stunt like that and stood there in the shadows naked, far too enticing to walk away from? "Where are your clothes?"

He shrugged. "I left them in my truck. That was what Adriana said nudists do here."

She should have known Adriana was behind this whole naked thing. She would— "That's why you called and asked to speak to Adriana. She put you up to this, didn't she?"

Cole shook his head. "I just asked her advice on the best way to get you to talk to me."

"Well, you got my attention, so talk." She folded her arms over her chest and kept her gaze focused on his face, slightly shadowed by his hat, which he'd donned once outside. To look anywhere else would make her melt.

Cole's focus was strictly on her. "I went to Orson."

She stiffened. "And?"

"I spoke to the deputy chief there. You wanted me to believe you back then, but I was still young and still believed everything my parents said, including that the town manager pulled in a favor and had the arson charge dropped because he was such a good friend of your family."

What? She opened her mouth to deny it, but Cole shook his head and held up his hand.

"I know. I didn't realize exactly how selfish my parents could be in regards to their reputation. That came later. But when you told me you didn't start the fire here and I found that so easy to believe, I started asking myself why I could believe in you now and not then. That's when the pieces came together for me. "

No wonder he was so sure she'd been guilty of the Orson fire, but she hadn't expected to hear he'd gone to the station. "Why did you go?"

"I had to know who or what had started the fire. You wanted

me to believe you about the Orson fire and the other night I came so close to lying to you, just to make you happy, but I couldn't do it." Cole broke eye contact and squinted at the desert. "I don't want to ever lie to you, even if it makes you feel better. It's not who I am." He brought his gaze back to her. "Can you understand that?"

She nodded. That she did accept. That was just who he was. And he had known who she was, which is why it had hurt so much that he'd believed the arson charge. "What did the deputy say?"

"That's the hardest part, and I'm hoping you can forgive me."

She didn't say anything, too afraid he was going to say that they found she had somehow caused the fire.

"Lacey, the fire was an accident, but you didn't cause it."

She dropped her arms as her body relaxed. Relief like she'd never known powered through her so fast, she leaned against the wall of the building for support. She should have called the station a long time ago, but a tiny piece of her was afraid of what she'd hear. Now it was truly in the past. "So who caused the fire?"

"I did."

"What? No. There's no way you would have started that fire, even back then."

Cole's eyes grew misty. She wanted to reach out to him, but his body language kept her at bay.

"It was an accident, but one I caused. Remember that night when you suggested whoever cleaned up fastest would undress the other?"

She nodded, puzzled.

"I wanted to undress you, so I threw the charcoals from the hibachi right outside the door, but they were still far too hot. We made love while they smoldered." He looked away briefly. "I was a little quick on the draw back then. But after I left, they continued to smolder, eventually setting the wall on fire." His face turned anguished. "With you inside."

"You wore me out and I fell asleep. My father called me, which is what woke me. I went to get out, but the door was on fire. My dad yelled at me to grab a blanket and cover myself. I did as he said and ran through."

Cole knelt at her feet and grasped her hips. "Lacey, I almost killed you. I could never have forgiven myself had that happened. You were my world and you still are. There will never be anyone else for me. Can you forgive me for wasting eight years that we could have been together?"

Even on one knee, he wasn't much shorter than her standing. She cupped his head in her palms and gazed into his bright-green eyes. "Cole, it was an accident. You had no way of knowing back then that that would happen. You weren't a firefighter, just a fledgling cowboy."

"And a clueless one at that."

She shrugged. "We all make mistakes, especially at that age, and to be fair I may have expected too much from you. But to lose eight years…" She shook her head. "I guess you'll just have to make it up to me for the rest of our lives."

Cole eyebrows rose. "Are you proposing to me, Lacey Winters?"

She leaned forward and gently kissed him. "I guess I am."

Giving a shout, he scooped her up into his arms and twirled her around. "Now that's my kind of proposal."

"Cole Hatcher, put me down this instant."

"My pleasure." He dropped her knees, but held her tight

against him. "Lacey, I love you. Always have. Always will. My answer is yes, I want to be your husband."

"I love you, Cole." She'd planned to say more, but his lips caught hers in a clothes-dropping kiss and she let him sweep her away.

~~~~~~

Cole woke. It was still pitch dark and Lacey lay by his side, sound asleep. At least it wasn't another one of her nightmares that woke him.

A thump, like a tennis ball hitting the outside of her casita caught his attention. That must have been what he heard. He glanced at the clock and groaned silently. It was barely after two. They hadn't fallen asleep until almost one. Carefully, he rose from the bed so as not to wake Lacey. After the celebratory dinner they had with the staff and their lovemaking, she was exhausted.

Thwap. Thwap. Thwap.

The sound was definitely something hitting the outside of the adobe structure. Quietly, he made his way to the living room and the sliding glass doors on the back side of the casita.

Thwap. Thwap. Thwap. Thwap.

Silently, he opened the slider far enough to squeeze through. Once outside, he could hear a muffled splat right after the thump on the front of the house. As he crept along the side wall, the crunching of tiny rocks beneath someone's feet sounded loud in the quiet night.

Thwap. Thwap.

He peered around the corner then pulled back and grinned. The teenager in him could appreciate the fun the college kid was having. Cole waited, knowing the perpetrator would be riveted to his handy work once he shot again.

Thwap. Thwap. Thwap. Thwap.

Cole stepped out. "I'm thinking the more you shoot, the longer it will take for you to clean this up."

The young man jumped at least a foot at his voice. It took all Cole's control to keep a stern look.

The college kid turned the paintball gun on him, his eyes wide with fear.

He walked a little closer. "That may hurt, but it's not going to stop me, so I'd think twice about shooting."

Indecision flashed over the kid's face while Cole contemplated the number of steps he'd need to tackle the young man to the ground.

The front door opened and they both looked at Lacey wrapped in a silky pink robe. "Cole, what's going on?"

Shit. So much for stealth. Cole ran for the kid.

The young man panicked and Cole almost tripped as hard balls hit his chest and stomach and burst across his naked body. He closed his eyes against the onslaught as one hit the side of his head before wiping the florescent green paint away and running straight out.

Ignoring Lacey's gasp, he leapt, bringing down the fast little son of a bitch.

"Let me go." The young man squirmed, making it difficult to keep a grip on him with the wet paint smeared over them both.

"I can take it from here." Cole looked up to see Hunter emerge out of the darkness.

"Great. Hope you don't mind getting dirty." Cole pulled the

kid up with an arm around his waist, thwarting any chance of escape. Green paint was everywhere.

Hunter pulled a zip tie out from his back pocket. Who carried zip ties with them? Then again, it made sense.

"I'll hold him while you do the honors."

Hunter nodded and quickly had the kid under control.

Lacey ran over. "How could you?"

The kid looked at her and shrugged. "I knew it was you. I saw you. You ratted out my friends, so you deserved it. Wait, I need a picture to show them."

Cole shook his head. "You can take a picture tomorrow after you're done washing all this off and you better hope it comes off or you'll be painting the entire house."

The kid pouted. "You can't make me do that. My father will—"

"What makes you think I'm going to tell your father? No, I think we will have you take care of this under the watchful eye of Detective Anderson before he actually brings you in and books you for trespassing and criminal mischief."

"And for attempted robbery." Hunter nodded to Cole then pulled the kid toward the main building.

Finally free to focus on his fiancée, he turned toward her and pulled her against his body.

"Cole! You're getting my robe green." She squirmed as hard as the kid had.

"Then take it off."

"What?"

In a second, he'd pulled the knot from the belt that held the ruined robe closed and slipped it from her shoulders. Her reaction was to plaster her body against him. He chuckled.

"Someone might see," she whispered to his chest.

"Lacey, we're on a nudist resort."

She just hugged him tighter.

"What do you say we go inside and wash this stuff off?" He grinned. "I don't think we've made love in your shower yet."

Her head came up at that and a small smile graced her dainty lips. "I'd like that."

He warmed at the thought of washing her. Growling, he scooped her up and strode to the front door.

Her squeal of delight was cut short when she groaned. "I hope he can get my casita clean."

Cole kicked the open door wide and shrugged. "Not to worry, you won't be living here long."

Her eyes widened before she slapped him with a cock-hardening kiss. By the time he reached her bathroom, he couldn't wait to thrust inside her. He stepped into the large, tiled shower and let her feet down then turned on the water.

Thanks to the cold night, it actually flowed chilly at first and Lacey glued her body against him.

"Are you cold?" He grinned, loving how she needed him for so many things.

She pulled back a little as the water warmed up and pressed her pointed finger into his chest. "Listen, Cole Hatcher, not everyone is hot like you."

He grasped her finger with his hand and brought it to his lips, watching her mouth as it opened in anticipation. "I'm only hot because you make me that way, Racy Lacey."

She smirked. "Well, if I'm a cowboy's match, you better get to work putting the fire out, Mr. Firefighter."

He moved her hand behind her and lowered his face until it was only inches from hers. "No, I don't think so. I want to see exactly how big this fire can get first."

She sucked in her breath before his lips claimed hers and she was lost to the flames only he could stoke.

EPILOGUE

Wiping her hands off on her skirt as she strolled back to the house at Last Chance Ranch, Lacey halted at the sight of Cole riding in on Sampson, a strong black quarter horse who wouldn't let anyone near him but Cole. She waited for him to bring the "Beast" as she'd nicknamed him, to a stop.

Cole jumped from the saddle, looped the reins over the fence and pulled her in for a searing kiss that had her forgetting everything but him.

When he finally lifted his head, he winked. "Missed you."

She looked at the sky then back at him. "You were only gone two hours. Did you find the spot?"

His grin widened. "I did. Do you want to see it?"

Her stomach turned somersaults in anticipation. "Yes, but I want to show you something first."

"Sounds good to me." He swept her up in his arms and headed for the ranch house.

"No, no. Cole Hatcher put me down." Really. The man had a one-track mind. It was amazing she could still walk.

His frown had her laughing as he released her.

"Tell you what. Why don't we pack a cold dinner and while we're out, we can make the most of our private time."

"I'll be holding you to that, Racy Lacey."

"Shh, Cole, your grandparents are around."

He stroked his finger over her cheek. "You're blushing again."

She swatted his hand aside and took his other one. "Come on." She couldn't wait to show him the progress she'd made with Angel. The dainty Arabian was finally starting to trust her. It would be hard leaving her to go back to Poker Flat for work tomorrow morning, but she loved her job too, so she'd just have to spend extra time with the horse when she came home.

She stopped outside Angel's stall. "Okay, I want you to stand right there. Don't move a muscle."

Cole tipped his hat at her. "Yes, ma'am."

"I'm not a ma'am…yet." But she would be soon. She looked at the modest diamond engagement ring on her left hand. Cole had wanted to buy her something expensive, but she'd chosen something more moderate to save money for the horses.

She approached the stall, then looked back to make sure Cole stayed where she put him. Assured he would behave, she called Angel by name.

The white horse raised her head and looked at her.

Stifling the urge to click her tongue, something the atrocious former owner must have done often, she instead kept her voice high. "Come show Cole what you like to do now, sweetie. Can you give me some lovin'?" She patted her own cheek.

The horse turned around, its brown eyes focused on her.

"Come on, Angel. You know I love you, sweetheart."

Trying to keep her heartbeat steady, Lacey focused on keeping her own excitement down and her breathing even.

The horse moved toward her and she patted her cheek again.

Angel brought the right side of her face, the side that hadn't been marred, to Lacey's right cheek and rubbed. Gently, Lacey moved her hand to stroke the horse up her nose and around her ears. "That's a good girl."

After a few minutes she turned away and looked at Cole. Pride was shining clearly in his eyes. "I'm glad you two are learning to get along. The minute I saw her I knew she was the perfect horse for you."

She raised her hand to her chest as her heart raced. "You mean she's mine."

"Only if you want her." Cole's look turned guarded and her heart ached for him. How many people had turned away his imperfect horses?

"That's the best gift anyone has ever given me."

His whole body relaxed as he grinned. "I knew you'd like her." He looked over her shoulder. "And it looks like she likes you, or at least your hair."

Lacey tried to turn around, but Angel had her braid between her teeth.

"Here let me." Cole walked over slowly, talking to Angel the whole time, finally coaxing her to let go. "There you go. I'm so proud of you."

She linked her arm around his waist. "I'm proud of you too. What you do here is amazing." She glanced up at him. "Are you going to miss the horses when Wade picks them up tomorrow?"

He shrugged. "Yeah, but I know they are going to a good home and it's one I plan to visit often."

"Not as a guest I hope." She squeezed him harder as they walked toward the house.

He chuckled, the vibration sending happiness through her.

"No, not as a guest. I don't think my wife will ever let me vacation there."

"You've got that right, mister." She laughed as he pretended to be scared. "You didn't tell me how it went yesterday with you and Sean. Did you manage to scare that fraternity house into toeing the line?"

Cole's grin was wide. "Yes, we did. You should have seen the look on their faces when the SWAT team showed up."

"Sean got the SWAT team to help, too?"

"Oh yeah. When I say Sean has no tolerance for stupidity, I mean it. That man had every one of those boys shaking in their boots. Then as a bonus, he arrested four for possession, three for having stolen property, and one for underage drinking. Then he told them he would send an undercover cop to the school to keep an eye on them."

Lacey stopped and Cole looked down. "What?"

"He's really sending an undercover in?"

"No." Cole shook his head. "But they don't know that. They'll be trying to figure out who it is for at least the rest of the year."

"Wow, remind me not to do anything stupid around that man."

He grinned. "You could never do anything stupid. You are way too smart for that. You're even too smart for me."

"I am not." She watched as his gaze moved over her to where his grandfather worked with a horse. She could tell Cole wanted to talk with him. "Why don't you go help your grandfather while I pack us up our dinner?"

He stopped and gave her a kiss on the forehead. "Thanks. Meet me by Sampson?"

She nodded and watched as he strode away, his ass stretching the material of his jeans nicely. If she had her way, those jeans wouldn't be on him long.

Anxious for them to be on their way, she ran up the steps to the porch, throwing the screen door wide, causing it to bang against the house. "Oops." She glanced out to see if it had spooked the horse, but it appeared intent on the two men.

She ran upstairs to Cole's room and grabbed a blanket from his closet. She hadn't fully moved in yet. She wanted their house to at least be started before she gave up her casita at Poker Flat. Right now, it was the only place they had complete privacy. She adored his grandparents, but she and Cole needed their own home.

Besides, the plan was once Billy made it through rehab, he would live in the guest room. It had been the carrot she'd needed to persuade him to get help, and Cole's willingness to give the man a second chance had proved to her exactly how special he was. Though he said it was Billy's "last chance", much like the name of the spread. She'd laughed when Cole's grandparents had explained the name for the ranch. They figured it was their "last chance" to follow their dream of raising cattle because they were so "old," but they were barely thirty-one at the time.

Back downstairs, she packed up a cloth bag with roast beef sandwiches and threw in a couple ice packs to keep the cans of lemonade cold. Then she walked back outside to find Cole waiting for her.

"You ready?" He took the items from her, securing the blanket to the saddle and pushing the food into a saddle bag. Then he cupped his hand and gave her a boost onto Sampson's back. As usual, the large horse pranced at having her up there, but Cole quickly mounted behind her.

In no time, they were riding across the ranch, the setting sun reflecting off the mountains, making them appear on fire with their orange glow. They hadn't ridden more than twenty minutes before Cole turned Sampson toward a hill in front of the long rise of a mountain. When they reached the top, she found them on a much larger piece of land than she'd expected. From this vantage point, she'd bet they could see the entire ranch, even his grandfather's house in the distance.

He pulled Sampson to a halt and dismounted. After helping her down, he pointed to a small creek that ran down the mountainside, though it was dried up this time of year. "This is Last Chance mountain, or at least that's what my grandfather calls it. And this area here my brother and I named Fire Hill because at sunset you can stand here and see the whole valley turn orange. What do you think about this for our new home? It's still close enough to the old house in case we're needed, but far enough away that we can have some privacy."

She looked around the little hill dotted with mesquite trees. "I think it's perfect."

He pulled her into his arms. "You're not just saying that to make me happy, are you?"

"No. I'm saying that because it's such a lovely spot. Of course, we'll have to get the road laid in first or the expense of bringing in construction materials will be twice as much. But I'm betting this is a good spot for a well, since it's at the base of a mountain. They'll probably still have to dig deep. This is Maricopa County after all."

"Whoa, we haven't even decided on the house plans yet and you're scheduling the infrastructure? You have to understand, Lacey, the money I had saved for this project has been raided a few times for vet bills so it may be awhile."

She frowned. "How long are you thinking?"

He looked over her head, a sure sign he wasn't comfortable with the conversation. But she had to know. Their finances would be tied together once they married.

"Maybe three or four years."

She shook her head. "Nope, I'm thinking a year tops."

"Lacey, you know I'd love to, but if I did that I'd have to turn away any—"

She pulled out of his arms. "Cole Hatcher, are we getting married or not?"

"Well, yes, but what does that have to do with our house?"

She sighed. "Everything. I know you're a cowboy and think you have to handle everything, but I'm an accountant. I'm not only good with numbers, I'm good with money."

"What are you saying?" His whole body tensed as if he expected her to knock him down.

"What I'm saying is that as Lacey Hatcher, my money will be added to your money and we will have enough to start building as soon as we decide on a design."

He stood rock still and her stomach tightened. Would he pull some macho bull poop over using her money? When he finally met her gaze, his grin was sheepish. "Do you think as my wife you could also work for no pay and take care of the books for Last Chance Ranch? I never was too good at math."

"Really?" She'd been itching to get her hands on them, sure she could help him make more money than he had been.

He took two steps to bring him directly in front of her. "I know you now. I know what you can do. I don't just trust you with my heart but with everything I own. I've always needed you. You fill in all my weak spots and hopefully, I fill in all yours. I want our marriage to be like our lovemaking, equal on all counts, completing each other."

She wrapped her arms around his neck. "Satisfying."

He ran his hands along her waist, across the sides of her breasts and up her arms. "Hot."

She stepped back. "Flaming hot." Slowly, she undid her button-down shirt and threw it over a mesquite branch. The pretty lavender bra she wore supported her breasts, but had a large hole in each cup where her areola and nipple were visible.

The air whistled out from between his teeth as he stared at her. "Shit, Lacey, that's beyond hot."

At his words her nipples hardened, making them stand out ahead of her pretty lingerie. "I want to see you, too."

Faster than a scorpion could strike, Cole had whipped off his t-shirt, his muscles tensing as his gaze riveted to her. Her hands itched to feel the hard planes of his chest again. The man's torso had more crevices and outcroppings than the mountain next to them.

Her folds moistened in anticipation of his gaze when she revealed what she wore below. Hooking her fingers in the waistband of her skirt, she pushed it down, stepping out of it and hanging it on another branch.

When she turned back, he was staring at her lavender panties. These too had a strategic hole. It revealed her small patch of blonde curls.

Cole growled as he unzipped his jeans and let out his hard cock.

In the next instant, he pulled her against him.

"Wrap your hands around my neck." It wasn't a request.

She did as told and shivered as her bare nipples pressed against his chest. Then he bent his knees and the tip of his erection found the lacy slit of her panties.

"I can't wait." His voice was strained. "I promise we'll go slow next time."

His words sent a thrill racing down her spine a second before he speared into her and raised her as he stood.

She gasped as her body lighted with fire and she wrapped her legs around him.

"Look at me." His words were gruff.

She raised her face to him, expecting a kiss.

Instead he gazed into her eyes. "I promise, I'll always believe you, always love you. You're my perfect match."

She quirked her mouth. "As long as I light your fire, I'll be happy."

His lips came down on hers, his tongue sweeping into her mouth. Then he moved his hips, fanning her fire, burning her up, like only he could.

For updates, sneak peeks, and special prizes, sign up to receive the latest news from Lexi at

http://bit.ly/LexiUpdate

Dear Reader,

I hope you enjoyed *Cowboy's Match*. I had so much fun writing this and quizzing my husband, former fire chief, on how fires start that aren't arson. It made for very entertaining dinner conversations. If you enjoyed Cole and Lacey's story, I hope you will leave a review, so others will find it.

And guess what? Their story continues in ***Christmas with Angel***. And the Poker Flat series isn't finished. Adriana, demanded her own happily ever after, so when my readers started to ask for it as well, I gave in and wrote ***Cowboy's Best Shot***. I hope you enjoy them all.

Always, Lexi

Read on for an excerpt from Christmas with Angel (Poker Flat Book 2.5 and Last Chance Book 1).

Chapter One

Last Chance Ranch, Arizona
December 23rd

Cole Hatcher added two pillows to the makeshift bed of sleeping bags on the hay. He'd unzipped each and spread them out so he and Lacey could crawl in together. Maybe if they could have a little privacy, they could settle their Christmas issue.

He'd pilfered all the snowflake decorations from the tree inside and hung them from the beams. In his mind, he'd envisioned it to look like it was snowing, but in reality, it looked like plastic, glass and felt snowflakes hanging from beams. Lacey would get it though. She couldn't expect more than this from her cowboy.

Adjusting the garland around the stall walls, he pulled over the small table he used for grooming the horses and placed it next to the bed. With a rag he'd grabbed from the house, he wiped it off and placed a bottle of wine on it with two plastic cups. "That should do it." His Christmas Eve present was ready, though a few hours early.

Stuffing the rag in his back pocket, he turned the battery-operated lantern to low and set it next to the wine. "Perfect."

As he headed out of the barn, the six horses in residence paid him no heed except for Angel. Her wary eyes watched him until he was out of sight.

Giving Angel to Lacey had been the best thing he'd done for

that horse, besides take her from her owner. She was so fearful of men that her bond with Lacey had grown strong.

Now if he could just get his fiancé onto the same page with him, life would be great again.

Cole strode across the dirt yard, the only sound to break the crisp night air, the two note call of a whippoorwill. The quiet beckoned him, but he needed Lacey to truly enjoy it. The house lights should have been welcoming but with his two cousins in residence, one baby, Billy and his grandparents, the four bedroom house was packed.

He took the stairs to the porch two at a time. Pulling back the screen door, he opened the heavy, ironwood front door. As he stepped in, he had to stop himself from stepping back out.

The baby cried upstairs while his two cousins, Logan and Trace argued. A door slammed on the upper level then Trace stomped down the stairs, yelling back over his shoulder, "I'll be watching the game with Grandpa if you come to your senses!" He nodded to Cole as he passed by.

Old Billy, who used to work and live at Poker Flat and had just spent two months in rehab for alcoholism, ambled through the front hall from the kitchen, a bottle of water in his hand and a smile on his face. The television in the living room clicked on just as Billy entered and the volume increased substantially.

Cole winced, the noise level and activity in the house was almost painful. Like Lacey, he couldn't wait for their own home to be completed, but it barely had walls and was far too incomplete for them to have the privacy and quiet they needed. Since Lacey had given up her casita at the Poker Flat Nudist Resort, they had nowhere to go…except the barn.

She was probably in their room where she always retreated right after dinner to crunch numbers, do research, or iron clothes for work. He ran up the stairs, excited to show her the present he'd arranged, and opened the door to the bedroom.

Lacey stood next to the bed, her deep pink sweater fitting her like a second-skin, wisps of blonde hair escaping her long braid. Her maroon skirt flowed about her, accentuating her delicate femininity. He still couldn't believe this hot woman was his. She had a basket of laundry dumped out on their bed, clean clothes strewn over the quilt and a small pile folded to her right. He walked straight to her and wrapped his arms around her waist from behind. "I have a surprise for you."

She stilled then sighed. "Is it ear plugs?"

He kissed her neck beneath her ear, loving how tiny she felt against him. "Even better."

She dropped his fire department t-shirt and turned in his arms. "Better is good." She lifted her arms around his neck. "Don't get me wrong. I love your family. There just seems to be so many of them in this particular house. And now that Billy's here, it makes it very cramped."

He looked into her light brown eyes that reminded him of amaretto. "You love my family? Even my parents?"

She lowered her lashes and stared at his chest.

Damn, he needed to wait to discuss that. Talking about his parents only brought up what his mother had done to break them apart. That didn't set the mood he wanted. He wouldn't press it now. "So aren't you a little bit curious about my surprise?"

She lifted her gaze to meet his. "Is this my Christmas Eve present?"

His family had always exchanged gifts on Christmas day, but maybe he and Lacey could start their own tradition. "Yes, just a few hours early."

She looked over her shoulder at the clock sitting on the nightstand. "Only three hours and seventeen minutes early. Should I wait?"

He started to grin but it turned to a grimace as his cousin's baby let out an ear-piercing wail. "You might be able to, but I can't."

At the sound of the baby's scream, Lacey buried her head against his chest. She lifted it to look up at him. "I could use a surprise right about now."

"Good." He kissed her on the forehead then let her go so he could take her hand. As he took a step toward the door, she resisted. "I thought you were going to give me a surprise."

"We have to go outside for this."

She pointed to the pile of clothes. "But I need to finish folding the laundry."

"Leave them. This is more important."

"Okay." She let him pull her down the hall.

When they got to the top of the stairs, he released her hand and stepped aside so she could descend first. Another screeching wail sounded from above, and they both picked up their pace. As he opened the front door, the television volume increased another decimal in the living room and from the corner of his eye he caught sight of Billy who had joined his grandfather and Trace.

Lacey stepped onto the porch and sighed.

No sooner had he closed the door than she placed her hand on his chest. "Do you hear that?"

He listened. The quiet was almost deafening until four hoots, sounding like a bouncing ball, broke the silence. "You mean the Screech Owl?"

She smiled slyly. "No, I mean the quiet."

He grinned. "Wait until you see my surprise." He took her hand and they walked down the steps toward the barn.

"I hope you didn't get me another horse. I'm very attached to Angel and I think she'd get jealous."

He shook his head. "No, it's not a horse. Luckily, I haven't had any calls this week. Maybe the Christmas spirit has people being kinder to their animals." He frowned at the thought of what else the Christmas season brought. "Now if we could just get Christmas tree fires under control, everyone could have a happy Christmas."

She squeezed his hand. "I've never understood the need for a live evergreen tree in the Arizona desert. It's so dry. If a person wants to smell evergreens, they can always go up to Prescott for the day or take a hike right here in our own mountains."

"You make the house smell great with those scented candles you use. I'm glad you found them in the glass jars."

She stopped at the entrance to the barn and looked at him. "Can you turn off the firefighter tonight and give me the cowboy who loves to save abused, hurt, and unwanted horses?"

He grinned sheepishly. "I'll try. Actually, your surprise is definitely from the cowboy." He winked.

Lacey's gaze roamed over him, and he couldn't help but count himself lucky all over again. To have found her a second time, at a fire no less, had been sheer luck. That she was just as dedicated to his horse rescue ranch as he was, was a bonus. Her wizardry with the finances had also improved their solvency. But to have captured her heart once more against all odds was the greatest luck of all. "If you keep looking at me like that, your surprise might have to wait."

She widened her eyes. "Like what?" She even batted her lashes.

He laughed and pulled her into his embrace. "I love you, soon-to-be Lacey Hatcher."

"I know." She stood on tiptoe to give him a kiss.

When she didn't deepen the kiss, he had to stop himself from lowering his lips to hers again. The open barn door was not the place to start making love to his woman. Reluctantly, he released her, but grasped her hand again.

After pulling the large door closed behind him, he led Lacey through the barn, passing the filled stalls until she slowed by Angel. He understood and let go, continuing toward the last stall, not wanting to disturb the bond between her and the rescued horse.

No sooner had Lacey turned toward the white Arabian, than Angel gave a soft nicker and walked to the stall door. Lacey pet the badly marred head, cooing to her like one would talk with a baby.

Cole never tired of watching their connection. He had almost given up hope that Angel would ever interact with humans again after the abuse she'd take from her former owner. That the horse came into his life shortly after he had found Lacey again made him think it was fate. Though the horse shied away from men, she completely trusted Lacey.

When Lacey finished, she walked slowly toward him, or was she sauntering toward him? Shit, his muscles tensed in anticipation.

She still wore her clothes from work, her long skirt swishing against her white cowboy boots. The sweater showed off her figure even if it didn't reveal even a hint of cleavage. It was hard to believe she worked at a nudist resort. He was thankful once again that the resort had a strict policy about employees keeping their clothes on during work. He would go insane if Lacey was supposed to work nude. On the other hand, because Kendra owned the nudist resort she was expected to be nude. He had no idea how Wade handled his fiancé being naked half the day. Cole couldn't do it.

But Lacey was sexy even with her clothes on, especially after a long day, when her braid had loosened and her messy wheat-colored hair made it look as if she'd just spent an hour in bed with him.

He watched her eyes closely as she approached. Her gaze was riveted to him and his chest puffed with pride. When she licked her lips, he had to force himself to stay still as every tendon pushed at him to move.

Finally, her gaze flitted to the stall behind him and her lips formed a pleased smile. "Oh Cole, it's the best present you could have given me."

He released the breath he'd been holding and opened his arms. "You like it?"

She walked straight into his embrace. "I love it."

"It might get a little chilly tonight."

She shrugged. "That's why I have you to keep me warm."

"Just to keep you warm?" He frowned. "I was hoping to start a fire inside you."

Lacey's short intake of breath had his cock taking notice.

She wrapped her arms around his neck. "You are as good at starting fires as putting them out."

"Only for you." He lowered his head and kissed her.

She pressed her body against him and pushed her tongue between his lips. He caught it with his own.

Every nook of her mouth was like new territory. He tasted the tartness of the wine she had with dinner and a flavor that was all Lacey. His hands roamed over her back, feeling her sweater slide against silk.

His cock hardened at the thought of what his Racy Lacey might be wearing underneath.

She pulled her lips away abruptly. "You have too many clothes on."

"I was thinking the same about you." He wiggled his brow. "I bet I can take my shirt off faster than you can." He let his arm go slack in anticipation of the race. They were always betting about sex.

She kept her arms around him. "And what does the winner get?"

"I'm thinking, choice of position." At his words, a shiver ran through her body, sending lightning straight to his balls.

"On the count of three. One. Two. Three."

No sooner had she dropped her arms than he reached back and pulled his flannel over his head. One button pinged across the stall, hitting the wood, as his face cleared the tail of the shirt.

Lacey had brought the sweater up over her head, but her face was still hidden.

Cole stared at the pale pink corset that cupped her breasts and accentuated her waist and hips. With her skirt still on, she looked like a saloon girl from the old west.

As she pulled the sweater free, she took a breath and her areolas peeked above their confines.

He swallowed hard.

"Are you admiring my new corset?" She smiled slyly, the vixen.

He shook his head as he traced a finger along the top edge of the satiny lingerie. "No, I'm admiring this." He pushed his finger inside the cup and flicked at the hard nipple beneath."

"But you like it, right?"

"I think it might require a closer inspection." He used his other hand to burrow beneath her other cup and lift the breast above the soft satin so the corset held it up for him to view her rosy tip. "Hmm, I'm liking it more and more." He performed the same readjustment on her other breast then stood back. "Now that's perfect." He stared at her hard nipples held aloft. "I really like it."

"I'm glad." Her lips formed a seductive pout. "But I lost the bet."

He reached out one hand and brushed his fingertips across her hard nipples. "Yes, you did."

Her chest rose as she sucked in a breath at his touch.

He loved how responsive she was. "I think it's time you took off your skirt so I can decide exactly what position I want you in."

She cocked her head. "And that must be determined by what I'm wearing underneath my skirt?"

He nodded. His soon-to-be wife never failed to surprise him when they crawled into bed at night. Her love of lingerie had him anticipating their alone time even during dinner. He was definitely the beneficiary of that little fetish. It didn't take much to get Lacey hot, but in the house, she had to keep quiet when they made love, and that took something away from the experience for her. Tonight, she could let go completely with no one the wiser.

Lacey untied the bow at her waist and pushed the skirt down to the barn floor before stepping out of it.

He was too distracted by the movement of her breasts at first, to understand her smile.

"So, what position would you like?" Her voice was teasing, a sound he hadn't heard in over a month.

This had definitely been needed. He lowered his gaze and raised his brows. "I can't decide until you take off that damn slip too."

She giggled, another sound he hadn't heard in a while. He needed to do something about that. The stress of building a house, working, caring for the horses with so much family around was too stressful for the only-child Lacey.

As she shimmied out of her slip, his jaw dropped and his cock hardened.

Read on for a preview of Cowboy's Best Shot (Poker Flat #3).

Chapter One

Adriana Perez pulled against the ropes that bound her wrists to the foot of the bed as lube ran down her crease. Being tied wasn't her favorite sex play, but a little was okay on occasion. She was just too far from being a submissive to really enjoy it.

The threesome staying at Poker Flat Nudist Resort was proving to be one of the better hookups she'd had in a long while. They at least had experience and appeared to be taking her challenge to them seriously—make her come.

She stood bent over, her wrists tied to the short footboard of the bed. The inside of the casita was lit by three lamps, leaving them all on display in the sliding glass door to her right. Not that it mattered, it was a nudist resort, and most of the guests were in their own casitas probably having their own fun. Besides, it was well after 1:00 a.m.—as that's when she'd closed the bar for the night.

The woman sitting on the floor beneath her had picked out two toys to use. The man behind her spread her ass as the cool liquid ran across her anal star and followed her flesh until it dripped to the floor.

The other man knelt on the bed, nipple clamps in his hands. Anticipation raced through her. She might actually orgasm this time without—

The cold metal of one clamp latched on to her right nipple. It was nothing new, but it did build some anticipation. He wrapped the chain over her neck and clamped the other metal clip to her left nipple. Her stomach tightened. This could prove enjoyable. As she moved her neck, the clamps pulled. Nice.

When he reached around her again, she held her breath, hoping he would tighten the clamps. He didn't disappoint. Her core clenched as the metal pinched her flesh. He sat back on the bed and nodded to the man behind her.

Finally, it would begin. She'd been a prostitute in her past life at a very exclusive bordello in Nevada. She'd done it not just for the money, but because she enjoyed sex. All kinds of sex. When she moved to Arizona to become Poker Flat's bartender, she found she missed the sex. Luckily, the resort opened and she'd been able to enjoy a few good lays.

The problem was that most of the people who stayed at a nudist resort were not into alternative lifestyles. They simply liked not wearing clothes. But occasionally swingers booked a couple casitas and they were always open to another woman.

The pressure of a hard cock against her anal hole had her grasping the footboard. The woman beneath her, Tina was her name, took that moment to press a vibrating dildo against her clit. "Ah, now that's what I'm talking about."

Tina didn't answer, probably didn't do anything her two Dominants didn't want her to do. When the vibration pulled away, Adriana glanced at her to see she'd turned on a vibrating bullet. There was more to sex than vibration, but she wasn't going to complain.

The cock behind her started to rub up and down her crease. The teasing motion had her pushing back. The smack of a hand on her ass stung. "Ow. What the hell? Don't spank me again or I'm out of here."

The man behind her chuckled. "That might be a little hard, tied to the bed."

She looked over her shoulder. What was his name? Tom? John? Something generic. "Don't push it."

"Whatever."

The man in front of her tsked and lifted her chin to look at him as he knelt before her. "Not smart to confront the most dominant."

"I told you, I'm not a submissive, nor do I want to be. You all agreed. Besides…" She paused as the woman slid the vibrating bullet inside her. Her sheath clenched it, happy to have the stimulation she craved. "You have this pretty thing under me. You don't need me."

The man behind her grunted. "True. But I am going to enjoy fucking your ass hole."

Despite his crudity, her core tensed. She used to serve a very classy clientele and they all enjoyed their own special kink. She'd just think of this as slumming.

"And I want to fuck that gorgeous mouth of yours." The man on the bed stroked her lips with his cock. "Would you like that?"

She grinned. This man she could handle just fine. She shot her tongue out and licked at the cock head in front of her. It wasn't long. She could easily take it in, but it was wide. She'd always been known for her big mouth. She smirked before nipping at the tip.

She opened her lips and sucked the cock halfway inside. The vibrating dildo made contact with her clit again, sending pleasure waves up to meet those being produced by the bullet, but that she could do on her own. It was the two men who were her hope for something more.

The rubbing along her ass crack slowed and she felt cool lube glide all around the cock head between her cheeks. She opened her mouth, allowing the cock in front of her to enter all the way. Being fucked from both ends had its own rewards.

Then the pressure built at her anal hole. She relaxed her muscles there as the woman pulled the dildo away from her clit and pushed it into her sheath until it met the bullet.

The man behind her grunted as he pushed in. "Fuck that's good."

The double vibration in her tight ass was making him happy. She turned her head to the side, keeping the cock in her mouth, and the nipple clamps pulled. That was better.

The woman beneath her must have realized the double vibration in her sheath wasn't enough and pulled it out to lay the dildo against her clit. Now, with the cock gliding in and out of her anal hole and the one in her mouth mimicking the motion, her tension finally built.

The vibrator against her clit started to circle and a tongue licked across her clamped right nipple. Yes, this was what she wanted. The orgasmic release that was like her own drug. The men in her ass and mouth started to lose control as they rocked into her. The tiny bites on her compressed nipple sent excitement colliding with the waves of tension building inside her vibrating sheath.

She was revved and ready but the sensations plateaued. Disappointment crept over her. She turned her head to the other side, just needing more, more feeling, pulling on the chain attached to her nipples. She needed someone watching.

Then in the darkness outside, a pair of black cowboy boots stepped into the light thrown from the sliders onto the patio.

Him.

Adriana caught her breath as every pleasurable sensation suddenly collided. Her orgasm hit hard, sending adrenaline racing along every artery, providing the satisfaction she craved.

She closed her eyes and the man on the bed came inside her mouth just as the one behind her yelled. The ecstasy left quickly, the moment gone as fast as it had come. It was as if she'd built up a tolerance to orgasms. Maybe she needed to lay off the toys for a while, dry out.

Yeah, who was she kidding?

She spit out the cock in her mouth and looked back to the patio. He was gone. She let her head drop, unconcerned that she was still tied and a bullet continued to buzz inside her.

The man behind her slowly pulled out. Instinct had her looking over her shoulder. "Don't even think about it."

He scowled, his hand raised to smack her ass. "I think you need to be taught a lesson."

"I don't need any lessons from you."

His tense face relaxed and he smirked. "Who said anything about me? Tina?"

The woman beneath her looked out at her Dom. "Yes, Sir."

"I want you to suck on this woman's clit while I wash up. If we make her come a second time, both Gary and I will fuck you at the same time. If she doesn't come, then neither will you...all night."

The woman simply nodded.

Adriana looked at him and raised her eyebrow. "A second time? No one's done that before."

"We'll see about that. Gary is going to fuck you until you come."

She hid her smirk by looking down. That wasn't going to

happen unless… She looked toward the sliding glass doors. The only way that would happen was if *he* came back on his rounds. And if he didn't? She rested her forehead on the footboard. She'd fake it. No reason to get sore for nothing. Besides, a part of her felt sorry for the woman. Yes, she was a submissive, but Adriana had to grit her teeth at the whole Dom/sub relationship.

The woman's tongue lapped against her clit, sending pleasing tingles up into her core.

Then again, it did have its advantages for her. She may not come, but she certainly planned to enjoy every sexual pleasure. And if the resort's mysterious security guard happened by again, she'd be ready.

~~~~~

Hunter McKade stalked away from the well-lit casita, his anger, always close to the surface, threatened to erupt. Why the fuck did he watch her every time? It wasn't as if he'd ever let himself experience that joy again, so why watch someone else have it? Self-directed fury tore through him, the hard-on in his jeans an annoyance.

He broke into a run up the hill toward the main building, letting the resentment rush through his body. He pushed his muscles, ignoring the cold night air so similar to Afghanistan. Habit had him scanning the distance for the lights of smugglers making their way through the mountains.

The Arizona desert remained dark. No enemy to avoid, no landmine to watch for.

When he reached the building, he curved left at the dirt road down into the ravine, his cowboy boots with their special rubber-coated soles and heels gripped the rock-strewn path, allowing him to continue his sprint. He hit the bridge over the creek, his boots silent in the quiet night, keeping his presence hidden despite the turmoil inside.

The winding path up the ravine wall was steep, but he refused to slow. He focused on his breathing, the burn in his thighs, the blood pumping through his body. When he made it to the top, he finally slowed to a jog, circling the three-walled steel garage big enough to fit half a dozen Abrams tanks. As he approached the open side again, he stopped and stepped inside, flicking on the overhead lights.

The rose-colored bulbs gave a warm feeling to the metal structure, a false impression.

To bring his breathing under control, he paced between the rows of parked vehicles. Wintertime at a nudist resort in Arizona brought in a shitload of people. He studied each vehicle, a habit he'd obtained since returning home.

He snarled at his thought, barely keeping his fist from slamming into a four-door sedan. He had no home anymore. No home, no life, no reason to go on. So why the fuck did he?

He turned the corner and slowed to a stop. The second vehicle down, a red SUV of the same make and model as the one that used to grace his ranch, was parked there, laughing at him, taunting him with its pretty paint job and dent-free body.

Fisting his hands as his heart raced, he moved past it, focusing on the light switch. "Hold it together, Hunter."

Why? Why should he?

He turned off the lights and shut out the image of the vehicle. He stood there in the dark, his breathing labored all over again, his heart speeding beyond its legal limit.

Poker Flat. The staff here. That was why he had to rein himself in. They didn't deserve the havoc he wanted to wreak. He focused on his boss and her fiancé, Wade. They were good people who didn't care that he was screwed up from the inside out. More on the inside than what the bombs had done to his outside.

His heartbeat started to slow. Lacey, the bookkeeper, was sweeter than apple pie, and Selma's cooking was a step above delicious. Jorge, the stable manager, took care of the horses like they were his children.

His body calmed, and he strode from the garage, heading back toward the resort. With the eruption of chaos averted and the usual darkness settling into his psyche and taking hold, he couldn't decide which was worse.

As he crested the ledge of the ravine, his gaze swept the entire resort. First, to the shelf with the stables and the newly constructed western main street. The figure of Mac stepped out of the stable manager's office and headed toward the western town. She made her rounds like he did his.

His gaze swept to the other shelf with the main building and casitas. The light still shone from one in particular. His cock responded as the image of Adriana Perez having sex with three people forced its way into his head.

He made his legs move, taking him down toward the ravine bed. The resort's bartender was taking a risk being tied up by people she didn't know well. He shook his head as his instinct to protect surfaced once again. He wished he hadn't chosen law enforcement before and during the army. Now he couldn't stop the serve and protect instincts, even if he cared less about himself.

His feet took him to the guest casitas again. He willed himself to stop before reaching the lit one. Adriana could take care of herself. She had yet to call him to evict an unruly customer at the bar, though he'd heard from his boss there had been a few since he'd been hired in October.

Then again Kendra could have exaggerated. Adriana was not a big woman like Mac. She was of average build for a female, but with large breasts, a thin waist and a round ass that had many of the resort's guests looking twice. But it was far more than her salacious body, petite nose, full lips and laughing brown eyes that caused people to watch her. The woman oozed sex appeal.

The way she walked, how she spoke, even her mannerisms said she was interested in sex. She was the kind of woman his mother had always told him to steer clear of and he had, until now. Now *he* was the one good people needed stay away from.

The light from the casita beckoned him like the light after death. He found it impossible to resist.

A quiet voice caught his attention, his senses always alert. He stepped farther into the shadow of the casita made by the weak moon as an older couple came down the walking path. They were naked as expected, but what was odd was there was no sound of flip-flops. Everyone wore those in the desert.

As they drew closer to the casita Adriana was in, they slowed and he was able to see they were barefoot. With snakes and tarantulas about, that wasn't a smart move. He was about to make himself known when the woman pointed.

"See," she whispered. "That's Dominance and submission."

The older gentleman with bright-white hair and a large gut nodded. "That's what I thought. So where does the masochism and sadism come in?"

The white-haired lady shrugged her pudgy shoulders. "I don't know. I think that's if they use whips and chains."

"That makes sense." The two watched the scene inside the casita, both barely blinking.

Hunter's own curiosity made him impatient to step around the corner, but he determinedly held his position.

"Oh wow. Honey, look." The woman squeezed her husband's arm. "He just put his penis in that other man's butt."

The husband didn't respond right away, his gaze on something entirely different. He glanced at what his wife mentioned, then pointed. "And that woman is performing oral sex on Adriana even while the man's penis is inside her."

The wife pulled his arm. "We better go, I don't think she'd like us watching."

The husband didn't budge, but he did chuckle. "We're talking about Adriana. The woman who walks around the resort nude when she's not on shift. I think she would love us to watch."

"Oh, I think she's coming."

The husband didn't respond to his wife's comment. Instead, they stood in silence as muffled sounds came from inside. When those sounds died down, the man had a hard-on.

The wife finally looked at him. "I'm ready now."

He grinned at her. "Me too. Let's go."

As the two ambled off, Hunter took a deep breath, confidant he'd made the right decision not to interrupt. But once they were out of sight, he stepped around the corner, this time careful to stay away from the light shining out of the sliding glass doors.

He expected to see Adriana untied and sitting on the floor recovering. He'd witnessed a number of nights when she didn't leave a sexual encounter until the sun threw a pink glow over the desert.

She wasn't untied yet. That bothered him. He'd only seen her tied once before and shortly after coming she'd been untied. Adriana would never be a submissive. A Dominatrix maybe, but never a submissive.

He watched the scene unfold inside. Adriana now knelt on the floor but her hands were still tied to the footboard. The other woman was on the bed, her legs spread wide, facing Adriana.

One of the men was missing, probably in the bathroom, but the other was arguing with Adriana. Hunter's gut tightened. This could get out of hand for her.

The man pointed to the woman on the bed. Adriana scowled at him, holding her hands up as far as they could go as she argued back. The man folded his arms and said something else.

Adriana shook her head, her chin coming up in defiance. The other man came into the room, a nasty-looking whip in his hand. Every muscle in Hunter's body came to attention. He curled his fingers into his palms. If this is what Adriana wanted, he'd hold his position, but if not…

He'd seen his fair share of kink while in the military. He'd even discovered his own captain with his dick stuck up the ass of one of his men. But it had been consensual and as far as Hunter was concerned, live and let live. He was in no position to judge anyone.

But he'd also seen rape and been prevented from interfering due to so-called "diplomatic relations," then been forced to bury the victim weeks later.

He narrowed his eyes at the scene before him, his weight already shifting to the balls of his feet. The dominant man now had the whip in his hand and pointed to the woman on the bed. Adriana lifted her tied hands again. The man raised the whip. She shook her head and spit on the floor.

He'd only seen her do that once, but she was furious at the time. He pulled the door handle as the whip came down.

Nothing happened. It was locked.

The impediment brought his rage to the surface. Picking up the stone planter at the edge of the patio, he threw it into the glass, his body coming through after it.

"Hunter!" Adriana's look of relief was all he needed to see.

Also by Lexi Post

Contemporary Cowboy Romance

Cowboys Never Fold
(Poker Flat Series: Book 1)
Cowboy's Match
(Poker Flat Series: Book 2)
Cowboy's Best Shot
(Poker Flat Series: Book 3)
Cowboy's Break
(Poker Flat Series: Book 4)
Wedding at Poker Flat
(Poker Flat Series: Book 5)

Christmas with Angel
(Poker Flat Series Book 2.5, Last Chance Series: Book 1)
Trace's Trouble
(Last Chance Series: Book 2)
Fletcher's Flame
(Last Chance Series: Book 3)
Logan's Luck
(Last Chance Series: Book 4)
Dillon's Dare
(Last Chance Series: Book 5)
Riley's Rescue
(Last Chance Series: Book 6) *Coming 2019*

Aloha Cowboy
(Last Chance Series: Book 5.5, Island Cowboy Series: Book 1)

Military Romance

When Love Chimes
(Broken Valor Series: Book 1)
Poisoned Honor
(Broken Valor Series: Book 2)

Paranormal Romance

Masque
Passion's Poison
Passion of Sleepy Hollow
Heart of Frankenstein

Pleasures of Christmas Past
(A Christmas Carol Series: Book 1)
Desires of Christmas Present
(A Christmas Carol Series: Book 2)
Temptations of Christmas Future
(A Christmas Carol: Book 3)
One of A Kind Christmas
(A Christmas Carol Series: Book 4)

On Highland Time
(Time Weavers, Inc. Book 1)
A Pocket in Time
(Time Weavers, Inc. Book 2) *Coming 2020*

Sci-fi Romance

Cruise into Eden
(The Eden Series: Book 1)
Unexpected Eden
(The Eden Series: Book 2)
Eden Discovered
(The Eden Series: Book 3)
Eden Revealed
(The Eden Series: Book 4)
Avenging Eden
(The Eden Series: Book 5)
Beast of Eden
(The Eden Series, Tolba: Book 1)
Bound by Eden
(The Eden Series, Tolba: Book 2)

ABOUT LEXI POST

Lexi Post is a New York Times and USA Today best-selling author of erotic romance inspired by the classics. She spent years in higher education taking and teaching courses about the classical literature she loved. From Edgar Allan Poe's short story "The Masque of the Red Death" to Tolstoy's *War and Peace*, she's read, studied, and taught wonderful classics.

But Lexi's first love is romance novels. In an effort to marry her two first loves, she started writing erotic romance inspired by the classics and found she loved it. Lexi believes there's no end to the romantic inspiration she can find in great literature. Her books are known for being "erotic romance with a whole lot of story."

Lexi is living her own happily ever after with her husband and her cat in Florida. She makes her own ice cream every weekend, loves bright colors, and is never seen without a hat.

www.lexipostbooks.com

Printed in Great Britain
by Amazon